Holly Smale is the author of *Geek Girl*, *Model Misfit*, *Picture Perfect*, *All that Glitters*, *Head Over Heels* and *Geek Girl* novellas, *All Wrapped Up* and *Sunny Side Up*. She was unexpectedly spotted by a top London modelling agency at the age of fifteen and spent the following two years falling over on catwalks, going bright red and breaking things she couldn't afford to replace. By the time Holly had graduated from Bristol University with a BA in English Literature and an MA in Shakespeare she had given up modelling and set herself on the path to becoming a writer.

Geek Girl was the no. 1 bestselling young adult fiction title in the UK in 2013. It was shortlisted for several major awards and won the Teen and Young Adult category of the Waterstones Children's Book Prize. The series has been published in 28 languages all over the world. Holly is currently writing the sixth and final book in the Geek Girl series, *Forever Geek*.

Follow Holly Smale on Twitter and Instagram:
@holsmale
www.facebook.com/geekgirlseries

For Helen, Kate and Lizzie. Without whom none of this would exist.

GEEK GIRL

SUNNY
SIDE UP

HOLLY
SMALE

HarperCollins *Children's Books*

First published in Great Britain by
HarperCollins *Children's Books* in 2016
Published in this edition in 2017
HarperCollins *Children's Books* is a division of HarperCollins*Publishers* Ltd,
HarperCollins Publishers
1 London Bridge Street
London SE1 9GF

The HarperCollins website address is: www.harpercollins.co.uk

1

isbn 978–0–00–819545–8

Holly Smale asserts the moral right to be identified as the author of the work.

Typeset in Frutiger Light by Palimpsest Book Production Limited, Falkirk, Stirlingshire
Printed and bound in England by Clays Ltd, St Ives plc

MIX
Paper from
responsible sources
FSC™ C007454

FSC™ is a non-profit international organisation established to promote
the responsible management of the world's forests. Products carrying the
FSC label are independently certified to assure consumers that they come
from forests that are managed to meet the social, economic and
ecological needs of present and future generations,
and other controlled sources.

Find out more about HarperCollins and the environment at
www.harpercollins.co.uk/green

Light (noun, adjective, verb)

/laɪt/

1   To make things visible or afford illumination

2   To set on fire

3   Pale or not deep in colour

4   Without weight

ORIGIN From the Old English *leoht* – light, shining or bright

1

My name is Harriet Manners and I am hyper.

Genki is a Japanese word that means *high energy, full of beans* or *peppy*, and I know it fits me perfectly because I haven't slept properly in six whole days.

Frankly, I haven't *needed* to.

I'm so super-charged, I'm basically a worker ant: grabbing hundreds of tiny minute-long power naps just to keep me performing as normal.

Trust me: I've got the data.

Thanks to the awesome new Sleep App on my phone, I've been able to track my nocturnal activities in detail. Statistically the average teenager needs 8.5 hours of decent rest per night, but – according to my sleep graphs – my deep sleep states have been dropping steadily for the last 144.3 hours.

Last night, in fact, I officially got no hours of proper sleep at all.

Not a single wink, let alone forty.

So it's pretty lucky that today I am firing on *all cylinders.* Giraffes can go weeks without napping, and I can only assume that I must be able to do the same now too.

Seriously: I am *buzzing.*

"*And,*" I continue, stabbing a finger at the magazine in front of me, "it says here that the tunnel includes six thousand tonnes of railway tracks, which is the same weight as two thousand elephants! Isn't that cool?"

I blink at buildings rushing past the window.

"At its deepest point, it runs seventy-five metres below sea level, which is the same as 107 baguettes on top of each other! Crazy, huh?"

Frowning, I click my biro rapidly in and out again with tiny *snaps* and make a little note next to this fact. "How many fish could you get into that space, do you think? Should I try and calculate it?"

"Oooh!" I add before anyone can answer, pointing

at a squat bird on a wire. "French pigeon!"

It's been a pretty exciting journey already.

Eleven in the morning, having departed London just two hours ago, and I've already completed three Sudoku puzzles, learnt three new foreign phrases and filled out my entire crossword book in pen. I didn't even bother pencilling it in first: that's how fired-up I'm feeling.

"*Plus*," I say, my jiggling leg bumping up and down repeatedly, "did you know that the Channel Tunnel is the longest under-sea tunnel *in the world*? Doesn't that just completely blow your—"

"Harriet?" a loud voice says from some way behind me. "Treacle-top, who the fiddlesticks are you talking to?"

I blink a few times.

Then – with a lurch of surprise – I spin round.

My modelling agent Wilbur is standing at the other end of the packed Eurostar train carriage wearing a fluffy green jumper covered in sequins, a pale lilac scarf covered with pink rabbits and neon-yellow trousers.

In one hand is a tray with two hot drinks on it and in the other is an enormous golden croissant.

9

Blankly, I turn to the seat next to me.

There's a large purple suitcase with a bright blue fake-fur coat draped over it and a wide-brimmed, orange-feathered hat perched on top.

Oh my God: you have *got* to be kidding me.

At what precise point in this conversation did Wilbur get up and go to the buffet car without me?

Exactly how long have I been publicly monologuing at a pile of accessories?

Ugh. Up to now, the jellyfish was the largest animal on the planet without a brain.

I think we have a new winner.

"Umm," I stammer as the young French couple behind me start quietly giggling. *Cover your tracks, Harriet.* "Hey there, Wilbur. I was just reading this magazine to the… uh… pigeon outside. He looked… lonely."

"Well of course he does, darling," Wilbur agrees chirpily, swinging into the spare seat opposite. "They're the rats of the sky, and who wants to date that?"

Then he holds out one of the coffees from the tray, pauses slightly and swings it back again. "On second

10

thoughts, poodle, I think you've had *quite* enough caffeine for one morning. You're starting to look like the victim at the start of a horror movie."

Typical. First you're given caffeine for the second time in your entire life, and then you're suddenly being cut off at the source with no explanation at all.

I might be shaking and sweating slightly from the end of my nose, but I am *fine*.

Wilbur puts a gentle hand on my still-kicking foot until it stops, calmly takes my still-clicking pen off me and puts the Eurostar magazine away, from where I'm now folding and unfolding the corners repeatedly.

"*Breathe,* possum," Wilbur smiles, patting my hand and proffering the golden croissant instead. "You've got this, munchkin, and you're not a baby mouse: there's no need to take in oxygen that fast."

I swallow and stare out of the train window as we rush past another French station and one more surge of adrenaline, fear, apprehension and excitement blasts through me. I never said what *kind* of energy I've been packed to the brim with all week, did I?

Nervous, mainly.

Include the significant quantities of central nervous system stimulating methylxanthine alkaloid I've imbibed this morning (caffeine), and I'm basically powering off raw natural chemicals like a sleep-deprived rocket.

I'm fine I'm fine I'm fine I'm—

"*Mesdames et messieurs,*" a calm female voice says as the Eurostar begins to pull into the enormous, cathedral-like Gard du Nord. "*Je l'espère vous avez eu un voyage agréable. S'il vous plaît que vous prenez vos bagages avec vous. Bienvenue a Paris.*"

And that's the *main* reason I haven't been able to sleep solidly for over a hundred and forty hours.

Why I've been lying on my back, staring at the glow-in-the-dark galaxy on my ceiling while my brain spins in tight little circles, like a dying neutron star.

Three little words, three long days, one huge city.

Yup.

I'm doing *Paris Fashion Week*.

2

You don't need to say it, by the way: I know what you're thinking.

How?

How did Harriet Manners – Destroyer of International Fashion Shows, Knocker-Over of Models, Sitter-Downer on Catwalks and Compiler of Compound Nouns – get selected to participate in *Paris Couture Fashion Week*: the most prestigious event a young model can possibly attend?

Well, I'm afraid I have no idea either.

Much like life's other great mysteries – such as how exactly a bicycle works and why yawning is contagious – there appears to be no real scientific answer to that question.

And it's basically what I've spent the last week trying to figure out.

Here are some things I do know:

- *Haute couture originated in France in 1858, and means High Sewing*
- *Every single dress shown has to be handmade, and just one can take up to two hundred hours to create*
- *There are only 2,000 potential customers for couture fashion, and most are based in India, Russia or Brazil*
- *Usually less than fifteen top designers worldwide qualify to show their creations in Paris, and the rules for participation are strict*
- *Haute couture dresses can cost up to £200,000 each*
- *Knowing these facts did not help me get this job.*

I definitely checked.

"Darling," Wilbur laughed when I suggested that my sartorial knowledge might elevate me above the thousands of other models also competing for the same positions, "one of my most well-known models – who shall remain nameless – once put a frozen chicken under the grill. I'm going to pause for a few seconds, to let that sink in."

There was a long silence while he closed his eyes tightly, bit his bottom lip and grabbed my arm.

"A whole, raw, frozen chicken," he repeated, slightly more squeakily. "Under the oven grill. And then couldn't work out why the legs caught fire."

Another pause.

Then he burst into peals of laughter. "I don't think intelligence is high on the list of qualities being searched for right now, banana-boo. This is not NASA."

By this point, Wilbur had been back from New York for just three days and had already swapped me with Stephanie for another one of his models, like Fashion Top Trumps except the opposite.

Let's just say there wasn't much of a struggle.

In fact, I'm pretty sure I saw her punch the air, shout WOOOHOOO then high-five the receptionist on her way out to lunch.

"Are you *sure*?" I said in dismay. "*None* of those facts

are relevant? Not even the one about how couture seamstresses are called *petits mains*, which means *little hands*?"

I'd studied with a very overexcited Nat all night.

The brain only has so much space: I'm positive that at least eight of my most interesting animal facts had been replaced with fashion regulations from the seventeenth century.

"Sure as a seasick sailor on leave," Wilbur giggled. "Just look angry but polite but distant but vague but smug in an untouchable kind of way and the world of couture is going to *love* you. Although you might want to switch your brain off for a few hours, pumpkin. Just in case you self-sabotage again like a baby lemming."

Which – when you're me – is easier said than done.

But I did my very best.

With a private black car specially booked for me and my *Infinity* portfolio tucked under one arm, I was driven to twelve different castings in London on one Saturday while my driver waited patiently outside (Wilbur said they were "taking no chances").

Carefully shepherded to *Dior* and *Balmain* and *Valentino* and *Elie Saab*; *Jean Paul Gaultier* and *Chanel* and *Versace*.

And with my rebellious brain switched firmly off, I walked up and down enormous, air-conditioned rooms: eyes flat, chin up, shoulders back. Cold and disinterested. Unimpressed and severe: very much like our headmistress just before an assembly about truancy.

Refusing to smile or chatter or ingratiate myself with relevant conversation openers or factual tidbits, and making no attempt to form connections with the people around me at all.

Suffice to say, it was one of my biggest personal challenges of all time.

And it totally worked.

Without my inherent personality, I didn't just get *one* high-fashion job for the week: I secured *three*.

Which was great – if a little hurtful – until last Saturday when I finally had to switch my brain back on and become…

Well, *me* again.

And then I went into meltdown.

There are 640 muscles in the average human body

and not a single one of mine has relaxed in the six days since.

"Darling-pie," Wilbur squeaks as the train doors *whoosh* open like a spaceship and he jumps out and spins around with his fluffy blue arms held wide like a gingerbread man, "can't you just *smell* it?"

I clamber down after him and inhale.

It's the end of January, and the Paris air is icy and fresh: underpinned with a faint whiff of train fumes, bread and the coffee Wilbur is guarding like the Crown Jewels.

"Winter?" I offer tentatively. "Odour molecules slow down when they hit a certain temperature, which is why cold air smells cleaner than warm air."

"*Fashion*," Wilbur exhales, before taking in another long, loud breath. "*High* fashion. *Exclusive* fashion. None of that high-street, something-for-everyone, we-can-all-be-part-of-it nonsense here."

He leaps a few steps forward like a fluffy sequined leprechaun and kisses a French bollard. "I'm back, baby," he sighs happily, wrapping his arms round it. "I'm *home*."

Swallowing, I glance at the unusually glamorous people getting off the train behind us – all sunglasses and fur scarves and heels and an aura of sophistication and inevitability – and another lurch of energy fires through me.

I'm trying to stay a paragon of positivity, the embodiment of enthusiasm: a shining example of sunniness in the face of all odds.

But how do I put this?

Wilbur might be home: in his spiritual heartland, at the place of his stylish and chic roots.

I am definitely not.

3

At least a *little* bit of normality has followed me here.

Invisibly, in the form of Nat.

My Best Friend, non-kissing-soulmate and owner of a very strong Wi-Fi signal, judging by how many times my phone has vibrated since we emerged from the Channel Tunnel.

The Caribbean White-lipped Frog buzzes so hard it can be felt twenty feet away, and I think Nat has the same natural skill for getting attention.

Beep.

ARE YOU AT PARIS FASHION WEEK YET? What's it like?! Is it amazing?! PICTURES! Nat xx

Beep.

Have you seen anyone famous? What were they wearing? Did you speak to them? PICTURES! Nat xx

Beep.

Need to see dresses and stages, front AND back. Try and find blueprints so I can copy at home. Nat xx

Beep.

PS PICTURES! :) :) Nat xx

With a small smile, I roll my new panda suitcase out of the station after Wilbur towards the taxi rank (it's a very *subtle* panda, by the way: shiny black with little white patches and mini ears by the handles, therefore not childish at all).

We wait in line while he talks on his phone.

Then we climb into a white taxi and start driving through the achingly elegant, taupe-stone streets of Paris: all long sash windows and delicate iron balconies and grey-tiled turrets stuffed full of painters and poets and authors wearing berets and discarding crêpes and starving for the truth of their art.

I'm presuming, anyway.

Finally, my phone beeps again:

Oh yeah, I forgot. Good luck with the job etc! Nat xx

I grin.

Obviously, in her enthusiasm for all things fashion, Nat momentarily forgot why I've been sent abroad: for gainful, paid employment in the modelling industry and not as her personal documentary maker.

For the first time ever, I remembered.

Stomach still lurching, I reverse the camera on my phone, take a quick selfie with my eyes crossed and my tongue out, then send it with:

PICTURE Number One! I hereby promise I shall document compulsively ;) Hxx

Then I turn back to Wilbur.

He's been tapping away on his phone with so much urgency since we got signal again, it looks like he's playing Whack-A-Mole with his fingers. I've never seen him so focused and professional, ever, in fifteen months.

It's slightly disorientating.

"*Et voilà*," the taxi driver says darkly, pulling up outside a small grey, sculpted building with an arched door and HOTEL written subtly on a canopy. "*C'est ça.*"

"Sar," Wilbur says without looking up.

The driver glares at him through the rear-view mirror, to absolutely no effect: my agent just keeps jabbing at his phone.

Nervously, I lean forward.

Time to break out my French language skills from school. Except maybe not the bit I remember about the lamp being on the table: I don't think that's going to help very much right now.

Or ever, actually.

If there's a lamp on a table, people can usually see it for themselves.

"*Mer-ci*," I say incredibly awkwardly, "*pour le –*" car lift drive journey… what's the word? – "*uh, vroom vroom.*"

Thanks for the vroom vroom.

Approximately 220 million people in the world speak French and, thanks to giving it up in Year Nine, I am not one of them.

"Mercy," Wilbur agrees distractedly as there's a loud *whoosh* from his hand. "Silver plate and whatnot. Comment ally views."

Clearly neither is Wilbur.

The driver taps his fingers on the steering wheel: obviously waiting for us to get out of his vehicle so he can continue with his normal, French-speaking day.

"Wilbur?" I prompt as the boot pops and – with some difficulty – I manage to clamber out awkwardly and drag my panda suitcase out of the back and on to the street.

Wilbur carries on typing.

"What's the first thing you want to do?" I peer through his window curiously. "Do you fancy grabbing lunch round the corner? Apparently they do an amazing *croque-monsieur*, which is a toasted cheese and ham sandwich and means 'bite-mister', although I'm not completely sure why. Or whatever you prefer. I'm totally ready for *anything*."

That's kind of the problem.

I've been *ready for anything* for six whole days: in adrenaline-fuelled, fight-or-flight mode for a hundred and forty-four straight hours.

A flash of black flickers in the corner of my eye and – with another *bang* of fear and nerves – I spin round quickly, but it's just a cat.

Calm, Harriet.

You're fine you're fine you're fine you're –

There's a pause, and then Wilbur finally puts his phone in his lap and glances up.

Then he starts laughing.

"Oh moon-puddle," he says affectionately, cocking his head to the side, "you don't think you're my only model at Paris Fashion Week, do you?"

I blink at him.

Yes. Obviously I do.

I've even got a little plan written out for any spare time we've got between shows: *Wilbur And Harriet's Awesome*

Parisian Fun-time Fashion Week Trip™. We were going to fit in a visit to *Le Cimetière de Chiens* (resting place of Rin Tin Tin and a heroic Saint Bernard called Barry) and definitely a trip to Shakespeare & Co, the famous bookshop where Hemingway and Fitzgerald used to hang out.

I've even sent the proprietors an email using Google Translate preparing for our arrival.

"N-no," I lie, flushing hard. "Of course not."

"My little box of tigers," Wilbur laughs, picking his phone back up. "I've got twelve models to manage this week. April's got a fitting at Versace in thirteen minutes and Joy needs introducing properly to Chanel because she had flu last week. I'm going to be busier than a fly with proverbial blue buttocks for the next week, or maybe green because blue's kind of *passé* this season."

I can feel myself literally crumple inwards.

I'm *way* too used to it being just me and Wilbur versus the high priests and priestesses of fashion.

"Although I *did* get to choose who I travelled with," he adds with a tiny smile, patting my fingers still clutching the top of the car window next to him, "and I picked my favourite baby-baby panda in the whole world."

Within seconds I've uncrumpled again.

I'm his favourite? *Yesssss.*

"So what do I do?" I ask, anxiety starting to pulse again. "How will I know what my first job is or where to go or how to get there or—"

"Do not fret, little frog-face," Wilbur laughs. "You've got nothing on 'til this evening. And I've had detailed instructions sent to your room, so just follow them to the letter, sugar-plum."

I unwind slightly. Now *that* I can do.

"I'll check in *sporadicment* by text," he continues with a grin, tapping on the driver's seat and gesturing forward with a regal flourish. "And don't worry, trunky-dunky – *gallons* of other models are staying in this hotel too. In fact, I *believe* you may even know one of them already."

He gives me a broad, unsubtle wink.

I open my mouth.

"Alley!" he cries before I can get another word out. "Ooooh reviews, my little ferret!"

And the taxi drives away without me in it.

4

According to perhaps debatable sources on the internet, human fingers are so sensitive, if yours were the size of Earth you'd still be able to tell the difference between a car and a house just by touching them.

It may or may not be true.

But if it is, the rest of me now feels equally responsive.

My whole body is quivering.

Every muscle is tense, my brain is jerking around like a pigeon and anything that moves in my peripheral vision feels like a flashing neon signal: LOOK AT ME!

A man in a big grey army coat crosses the road and my stomach lurches. A girl with dark curls emerges from the corner and I double-glance at her.

A car horn honks and I jump.

I believe you may even know one of them already.

WINK.

What was *that* supposed to mean?

WHO?

Jittering, I grab my panda suitcase from the kerb and feel my now-sweaty hands slip on the handle. My heart is starting to hammer like a tiny, enthusiastic tap-dancer.

Breathe, Harriet. In and out.

You've done it more than 118 million times already this lifetime: a few more can't be that hard.

With a wobble, I wheel myself through the hotel doors into a small but perfectly neat and glossy reception. There are white lilies in a huge glass vase, marble floors, and candles arranged neatly in groups on shelves.

Flute music is playing in the background through discreet speakers and there's a cut-glass bowl of white matchsticks on the counter.

It's calm. Serene. Beautiful.

And its ambience has absolutely no effect on my current mental state whatsoever.

"Hello," a neatly dressed lady with a short black crop

says, smiling politely. "Welcome to *L'Hotel Bisou*. And how was your trip?" Her accent is fluid and musical, lilting with perfect, clipped Frenchness.

Bisou... Bisou... Bi—

Wait, Hotel *Kisses*? What kind of horrible romantic name is that for an official place of accommodation?

Then with a frown, I glance down in disappointment at my stripy black and white jumper, thick black tights and blue denim shorts.

I really thought I'd nailed French Casual Chic today, but as the receptionist knew I was English before I even opened my mouth, maybe I shouldn't have got rid of the jaunty beret Nat told me was overkill after all.

"It was good," I say, handing her my passport and glancing quickly to the side. A very beautiful tall Japanese girl glides by in flat black pumps, a tight black jumper and skinny black jeans. "Thank you very much."

There's a movement in the corner of my eye and I swing to the right. An auburn-haired girl with sharp cheekbones and slanted, cat-like features swings past in a blue dress and flat white trainers.

"I am so glad," the receptionist says warmly, taking my passport and clicking a few buttons on her computer. "*Merci*."

I nod, swinging round again.

An incredibly good-looking boy with a sloping nose and white hair slinks by, talking to an even better-looking boy with black skin and pouted lips and a shaved head.

"Thank you," I say distantly, heart pounding harder.

"And is this your first time in Paris?" the receptionist says, handing back my passport.

"I've been here before," I say distractedly, whizzing round again. A tanned blonde girl has just entered the door behind me. "With my parents. On… holiday."

Not *strictly* true: Annabel was here years ago when one of her French clients was going through a divorce, so Dad brought me to visit her for the weekend and we spent forty-eight hours straight consuming sugar in fifteen different forms.

"Ah," the receptionist nods, glancing at the form that says INFINITY MODELS at the top of the payment slip.

"Paris Fashion Week will be very special this year, I think. Your room key, *mademoiselle.*"

I nod again as she hands over a plain fold of white cardboard with my room number written on it and a plastic key-card inside, then start heading as fast as I can towards the shiny gold elevator.

I don't think I can handle seeing one more person who I might happen to know all too well right now...

Go go go go go go.

"Thank you!" I call over my shoulder as I hit the button three times in a panic.

Come on come on come on...

"*Et aussi,* you are in luck!" she calls after me. "Paris Men's Fashion Week does not end until tomorrow. If you hurry, you will be able to see some of the boys too!"

Ping.

And as the shiny brass doors slide smoothly open, my very worst fear is confirmed.

Because there's *another* reason why I haven't been able to sleep for an entire week.

Or eat or read or focus on my schoolwork.

Since last Saturday afternoon at precisely 2:12pm, when I discovered what Nat had been carefully keeping from me for weeks: that Paris Women's Couture Fashion Week overlaps with Paris Men's Fashion Week by two whole days.

And that those two days are *now*.

Which means that every top male model under the sun is going to be in Paris for the next forty-eight hours.

So it doesn't matter that Nick Hidaka officially quit the fashion world last autumn and went back to Australia; that I broke my own heart on Brooklyn Bridge so that he could have his freedom back.

It doesn't matter that I'm pretty sure he hasn't returned to modelling, even though I haven't asked or checked because I'm too scared of what I'd find out.

Or that he's *highly unlikely* to be in Paris this week.

I'm still like a rabbit caught in the headlights: frantically wondering which way to run.

The odds of getting struck by lightning are one in 700,000, but that still means 24,000 people are killed by it every year.

The chances of winning the lottery are approximately

one in fourteen million, and yet ninety-nine per cent of winners continue playing once they've hit the jackpot in the hope that they will win again.

And the chances of dating a supermodel are one in 88,000, and yet I somehow beat those odds for over a year.

So I can put the love of my life in a box in my head and push it away as firmly as I like, statistics still know better.

A chance is a chance, however small.

Nick could be in Paris.

And I have absolutely no idea how to lock *that* fact up.

5

I'm just going to have to try.

Without putting too fine a point on it, I've got quite enough to worry about for the next few days without adding ex-boyfriends to the mix.

Especially given that:

a) I'm so discombobulated I've just gone to the wrong floor in this lift, three times

b) My suitcase got stuck in the brass doors and in my urgency to escape, I ripped one of Pandora's ears off

c) I've totally named my luggage

d) I just realised I left my spare knickers, hairbrush, toothpaste, toothbrush and deodorant in a neat pile next to my bed in England.

Oh and:

e) *Last time I went abroad for a fashion job, I performed so badly that they had to shoot the entire commercial again with a different model.*

This time I *really* need to focus.

With a surge of extra adrenaline, I check that Nick's firmly in the box in my head and metaphorically sit on top of the lid, just to make sure.

Then I click open my hotel-room door.

It's tiny like the lobby downstairs, but so pretty: the bed is pure white, smooth cotton, there are brightly coloured pillows strewn across it in blues and pinks, and the large bedside window looks straight out on to a street unsurprisingly lined with horse chestnut trees (Paris has more trees than any other capital city in Europe).

On the walls hang artfully spaced purple paintings and there's a small lilac-fringed tapestry directly above the bed.

There's a flat-screened television on the opposite wall,

and a teensy bathroom that's made almost entirely out of marble and doesn't have a father, stepmother or baby in it or smashing on its door, asking when you're going to finish as if you have any kind of control over the timing of body functions.

In other words: *it's all mine.*

I give a little squeak of happiness.

Grabbing my phone, I take a quick series of photos of the room.

I ping them all to Nat.

Then I send a quick text to the rest of Team JINTH, now getting on with their Saturday without me. Jasper, serving coffee and sarcasm at the cafe his dad owns. India, driving her purple car around town.

Toby…

Probably constructing some kind of home-made Batmobile out of cereal boxes.

Paris is great! I'VE GOT MY OWN BATHROOM! CAN YOU BELIEVE IT?! Harriet x

Then I grin and fling myself in a wide, floppy star shape on the bed.

It's very important to focus on the *bright side* over the next few days. To stay sunny and optimistic, no matter how stressed or anxious I get. After all, I am insanely lucky to even be here in the first place.

In just a minute, I'm going to get up and get on with some of *Wilbur And Harriet's Awesome Parisian Fun-time Fashion Week Trip™*: even if I have to go it alone.

I can go to Père-Lachaise, the most visited cemetery in the world, and pay my respects to the graves of Oscar Wilde (for me) and Chopin (for Annabel) and Jim Morrison (for Dad).

I'll wander around *La Cité des Sciences et de L'Industrie,* Europe's largest science museum, and check out the scale model of the *Ariane* space shuttle: perhaps carefully examine the exhibition of Charles Darwin and the original manuscript of *On the Origin of Species.*

I can walk through Montmartre, which was occupied by Russian soldiers during the Battle of Paris in 1814 and Jasper says has been filled with many artists through centuries, like Matisse and Picasso and Degas and Dalí.

Painting long-legged elephants and ballerinas and white horses and melting clocks and butterfly ships and heads on sticks and tigers roaring out of the mouth of a fish and –

And swans that turn into elephants that turn into swans that turn into elephants –

And elephants –

And –

6

I awake with a jolt.

For a few seconds, I have no idea where I am. It's dark, the bed sheets don't smell of me, there are unfamiliar traffic sounds and no five-month-old sister in the next room, either giggling or screaming the house down.

Then it slowly comes back.

I'm in Paris. I'm in a hotel. I'm fully dressed with my trainers on and my phone in one hand. It's Couture Fashion Week and I'm...

I'm supposed to be somewhere.

DINGOBATS.

Sitting bolt upright, I flick on the bedside table lamp and blink around the room. There's a large gilt mirror on the

45

opposite wall and in it I can see that my fringe is standing upwards, my eyelids are pink and crusty, there's an imprint of lace cushion on my forehead and a big spot erupting on my chin.

Stuck to my left cheek is a large, damp square of cream card, covered in gold writing.

Quickly, I pull it off and read the note hastily scribbled on the back.

Monkey-moo Manners,

Your first job is to P-A-R-T-Y! Pumpkin* to arrive for Cinders at 7:50pm sharp.

REMEMBER TO WEAR DRESS!

PS – don't pick your spots. We can ALWAYS TELL.

F-G Wilbur

*Black Citroën

46

Panicking in earnest now, I glance at my watch.

A 2008 Texas University study found that early risers were significantly more likely to get a high grade in class than people who sleep in late.

I have no idea what they discovered about people who get up at dawn and then snooze until 7:45pm in the evening, but I'm hoping it's good because I am essentially now nocturnal.

Also, at no point in any fairytale did Cinderella have to transform *herself* into party-worthy appearance.

Adrenaline surging again, I take a quick photo of the invitation and send it to Nat.

Almost immediately, I get a reply from Nat.

So *jealous*! MAKE SURE YOU WEAR THAT DRESS! :)

I roll my eyes: does she think I'm going to a Paris Fashion Party dressed like *this*?

I am not a *total* fashion rookie.

Then I start ripping apart my suitcase.

It's very much a packing of two halves: like the luggage version of Jekyll and Hyde.

One side looks like a clothing grenade has exploded inside a rainbow and then a rat has tried to reorganise the chaos with its teeth. There are green socks knotted up with yellow leggings tied up with blue-and-purple T-shirts and covered in red jumpers: all of which are so crumpled they're now unrecognisable as anything a sane person would want to wear.

The other side is beautifully arranged and smells faintly of vanilla. It has a black velvet make-up bag tucked in one corner and a neat package wrapped in soft pale yellow tissue, secured with ribbons.

Nat and I spent all last night packing together.

Guess who did which side.

Quickly, I switch the light on in the bathroom, grab the make-up bag, unzip it and lob the contents into the empty sink.

As fast as I can, I wash off the ink from the invitation from my face and scratch off tiny flakes of gold. I smear some foundation across my nose with my fingers, cover the pulsing zit with an inch of concealer, rub on a little gel blusher and oh-so-slowly apply two layers of mascara (Nat informed me that it's better to arrive late than blinded by a small furry stick).

I break a *L'Hotel Bisou* plastic comb in half trying to pull it through my tangled hair, give up and shove my unruly frizz into a very literal top-knot. Speedily, I scrub my teeth with the world's smallest free hotel toothbrush.

Then I race back to my suitcase, carefully take out the precious tissue package and open it on the bed.

And immediately suck in my breath.

There's no other way to put it: this dress is magnificent. Spectacular. Majestic. Awe-inspiring. *Haute Couture* in every possible sense: handmade, hand-cut and hand-sewn, the very Highest of Sewing.

The pale, lime green strapless bodice graduates to a darker, moss green round the waist and then falls to a jagged dark jade colour at my knees. The dress is edged with delicate green lace dyed in subtly different shades, creeping prettily up my throat, along the top of my shoulders and down my back.

49

It makes me feel a bit like an elegant walking rainforest, in a really good way: all I need now is a panther on my shoulder and a tiny magenta parrot nesting in my hair.

And – as it's been designed for me, coloured for me and fitted to me – it suits me perfectly.

Without a shadow of a doubt, I am *so lucky.*

Beaming, I slip out of my travel-weary clothes, tug the Work of Art on as carefully as possible and zip it up. I stand in front of the mirror, take a triumphant photo and send it to Nat, grab the petite beaded green bag Nat thankfully packed for me and sling it over my shoulder.

I turn my phone on silent and throw it to the bottom with my invitation card.

Then I start rummaging through my suitcase for the rest of the outfit.

I rummage a little harder.

Then a bit harder.

Until – as I start desperately hauling out the contents

and distributing them around the room like a hamster energetically rearranging its nest – it finally hits me.

No no no no *no*...

"Don't forget these," Nat said last night as I rocketed around the internet, collecting interesting facts about Paris. "Harriet?"

"There is only *one* STOP sign in the whole of Paris!" I told her, bending over my laptop. "But one thousand seven hundred and eighty-four bakeries! Amazing!"

"Harriet."

"They have more dogs in Paris than they do children! More than 300,000!"

"Harriet."

"And France is the most visited country on the planet! I did not know that. Did you know that?"

"HARRIET, LOOK AT ME."

I blinked and turned round.

My best friend was sitting on the edge of my bed, holding a pair of pale green heels in the air. "What are these?"

I narrowed my eyes. *You can do this, Harriet.*

"Kitten heels?" I guessed confidently.

Nat's nose twitched.

"Mary Janes? Cones? Pumps? Wait, I've got that list you gave me somewhere."

"*Your shoes*, Harriet," Nat sighed. "Or maybe I should say, *The Shoes* I'm lending you to wear with that outfit. Put them in your suitcase right now."

"I will in a minute," I nodded, turning back to my laptop. "I've just got to print these facts out. And maybe laminate them."

"*Now*, Harriet."

"Just shove them in the pile with my hairbrush and toothbrush and deodorant. I'll have to use *them* before I leave tomorrow morning, so I definitely won't forget."

Nat frowned. "But what if you skip basic hygiene?"

"I'm an international *model*, Nat," I laughed, rolling my eyes. "How unhygienic do you think I am?"

We have our answer.

My posh shoes are currently over two hundred miles away: next to my bed, along with everything else I didn't even look at this morning, including dental floss and mouthwash.

Heart sinking, I glance around my tiny hotel room: the only footwear option I have is the shoes I wore here. My bright pink trainers with orange stripes and pale blue laces.

I have to hide them from Nat when she comes round in case she destroys them.

Now I may have to hide *me.*

Sighing, I tug the trainers on with my beautiful couture dress.

I take my deepest breath and try not to think of what might lie ahead of me.

Or *who.*

And I prepare to meet my fashion-fate head on.

1

Goosebumps are fascinating.

Believe it or not, they're an evolutionary hangover from our days as monkeys. Just like most land mammals, humans have tiny muscles round the base of each of our body hairs, and thousands of years ago when we were cold they'd tighten to fluff up our fur coats, trap air and make us warmer.

Likewise, when we were scared or anxious, they'd fluff up to make us look bigger and scarier to any potential predators.

Obviously most of us have much finer and fewer body hairs now (apart from Mr Harper, my physics teacher), but our follicles haven't registered that yet: they still try to defend us and that's why when there's an external threat we get bumps all over.

It's called *horripilation.*

Which is quite fitting, because – as the black Citroën I'm in pulls up to the Parisian kerb and I open the door – I'm suddenly both so terrified *and* cold I'm horripilating all over in tiny, prickly bumps.

Thank goodness I shaved my legs last night.

Or now I'd literally be Mr Tumnus from *The Lion, The Witch and The Wardrobe.*

"*Merci,*" I say politely to the taxi driver, leaning out. I finally remembered the right phrase on the journey: "*Pour le* journey…"

And that's it.

Because as my foot touches the ground all speech – in any language – evaporates completely.

Directly in front of me is the Seine.

An inky expanse of black water twists in both directions, glittering with a rainbow of white, yellow, blue and red lights reflected from the banks.

To my left is *Le Pont D'Austerlitz*: a pale-grey stone bridge with five arches, vaulting its way across the river.

In front of me, the bank is lined with spiny, leafless trees from the edge of the *Jardin des Plantes* and accompanying zoo. If I turn to the right, I can just see *Notre Dame,* crouched on its island in the middle of the water: lit up and sparkling like a beautiful, domed frog.

A little down the river is the Eiffel Tower: tall and iron, blue-lit and covered in sparkly lights, like the world's most industrial Christmas tree.

But, as stunning as all of this is, that's not what's sucked the French right out of me.

There's also a boat.

Shiny and white with mahogany flanks and *Superbe II* written on it in gold scroll, anchored to the pavement directly in front of where my car has stopped. It's lit from within, violin music is already playing, glamorous people are collecting on the deck and there's a tinkling of glasses, of cutlery, of heels.

Running up to and over the gangplank is a bright purple carpet and two purple silk ropes.

And on either side of these luxurious barriers are people who look much cosier than me.

Dozens of them: wrapped up in warm puffa jackets, wearing scarves and hats, crammed together in a tight mass of bodies like emperor penguins.

And every single one of them is holding an enormous high-tech camera.

I swallow uncertainly.

It takes twelve hours for the body to fully digest food, and I have a feeling I'm going to see my Eurostar croissant again sooner than I thought.

What the— Who the—

"Harriet!" one shouts, suddenly whipping round.

Another spins. "Harriet from Baylee! Over here, Harriet!"

"Yuka Ito girl! Look this way! HARRIET!"

And – in a flash of glare and sound – the crowd goes bonkers.

8

All over the world, Paris is known as The City of Lights. This is for two key reasons:

a) It had a leading role during the Age of Enlightenment, a philosophical movement that dominated Europe in the 18th century.

b) Paris was one of the first cities to adopt gas street lighting, and was illuminated in the 1860s by 56,000 lamps.

Apparently most people also find all the electricity and candles of Paris very romantic, but that's more anecdotal than factual so I'm discarding that bit of received wisdom, thank you very much.

I can now add a third reason to the list:

c) They have *a lot of paparazzi.*

Within seconds of stepping out of the car, I'm temporarily blinded. Dozens of white flashes are clicking and fire-working in every direction; people are yelling at me; hands are being waved. And my name is being called, over and over again.

Harriet! Harriet! Harriet! Harriet!

For a brief moment I almost turn round, get back into the taxi and tell the chauffeur to drive 469 kilometres all the way back to London. There are approximately 3,875 models working the catwalks around the world in any given season: why the bat poop am I being recognised?

How do they know who I am?

Then it suddenly hits me. I haven't been anywhere apart from school since the enormous Yuka Ito campaign ran last autumn, along with the simultaneous Baylee photos and the *Vogue* adverts. The general person on the street – or in the classroom – may not care who I am, but this is the world of *fashion.*

And they do, apparently.

Gulping, I take a miniscule step forward and thank every single one of the hundred billion stars in our galaxy that I'm wearing comfortable trainers and not slippery green kitten heels.

Then I brace myself.

This is the best thing that could possibly have happened, and as terrifying as it is I have to make the most of every single second.

"Harriet!" somebody yells as I step on to the carpet and a couple of girls wearing purple walk past me. "Over here! To me, sweetheart!"

Taking another step forward, I turn slightly and stand with one hand on my hip and my shoulders back: my posture as straight and stretched out as possible, the way Nat instructed me.

There's a series of blinding flashes.

"Baylee girl! This way! Harriet! *Harriet!*"

Holding my chin up, I swing the other way and try to keep my smile mysterious and relaxed, my eyes enigmatic, my facial expression serene and above it all. As if I'm not shaking with nerves inside.

Another blaze of lights.

"Who are you wearing tonight, Harriet?" somebody shouts as a few more purple-clad guests wander past, pausing to glance over.

I stare at them in horror. *Who am I wearing?* "I'm pretty sure the silkworms didn't have names," I blurt, "but they're probably from China."

Now I feel *awful*.

"Which *designer*?" somebody else yells. "Who made the outfit?"

Oh. *Oh*. Whoops.

I hold myself as still and as elegant as possible.

"Tonight," I amend loudly and clearly, "I am wearing a beautiful *haute couture* dress by *Nat Grey*."

Then I twirl like an emerald hummingbird in the green dress my best friend made especially for me.

We were both optimistic that somebody might – at some point – take a photo of me wearing it, maybe in the background. In our wildest dreams, we couldn't have hoped for *this* reaction. Whatever happens – however weird it feels – I have to try and milk it: making this dress took Nat *months*.

63

"She's an up-and-coming British designer," I add proudly, taking a few more steps towards the journalists and spinning round a little bit more so the skirt flares out. *I'm doing it, Nat!* "She's the next Big Thing. HUGE. Bigger than… erm… big. *Monolithic.*"

Another few flashes.

"And the shoes?" somebody yells as a few more boys and girls cross my path. "Where are the shoes from?"

Sugar cookies.

I take another few steps up the ramp towards the boat. If Nat finds out she's being blamed for my horrific combination of fluorescent-trainers-and-beautiful-gown, eleven years of friendship are going straight down the toilet.

Again.

"These are… uh…" I pose carefully with my hand on the boat rail while I scrabble for an answer. "A well-known British… high-street brand, who also specialise in many…. uh… other areas. It's important to mix *affordable* style with *aspirational.*"

Tesco. They're from Tesco.

I got them on our weekly food shop and popped them under the bread rolls and boxes of Pop Tarts.

A few more camera flashes.

Finally, I manage to get to the top of the ad-hoc runway where there's a big purple backdrop with luxury car logos emblazoned across it in silver. Then I spin confidently to face them. I'm so delighted, I'm starting to buzz and vibrate all over.

Wilbur was right, partying really *is* a job.

And I am surprisingly *good* at it.

Flushed with success – mostly Nat's, but a tiny bit of my own too – I turn and do a final flourish with my hand, a bit like the Queen.

"Thank you!" I call, slightly carried away now. Beaming, I hold the bottom of my skirt out and curtsy to the left. "*Merci!*" I curtsy to the right. "*Merci,* my friends!" I hold my arms up in the air. "I'll be here all ni—"

A hand grabs me from the side.

"What," a woman hisses as I'm yanked unceremoniously behind the door of the boat, "the *hell* do you think you're doing?"

9

Honestly, if I had a penny for every time somebody has asked me *What the hell do you think you're doing?* I wouldn't need to model at all.

I'd have paid for university already, and probably a Masters, PhD and some kind of internship on a professional archaeological dig in Egypt too.

But usually I have *some* idea of the answer.

This time, however, I'm at a total loss.

A very small, sharp-featured woman with a bleached-white bob, purple crop top and perfect purple lips has dragged me in silent rage into an ominously empty back room of the yacht and is glaring at me intensely. I have literally no idea why.

I arrived on time for once, right?

I didn't fall over or break anything, did I?

I obeyed Wilbur's letter to the letter, didn't I?

Unless... Oh no, is it the spot? Am I in trouble for looking like I have a unicorn horn on my chin again? Can she see I've been distractedly prodding it in the car on the way here? Am I in the wrong place?

Whose party *is* this anyway?

"I'm so sorry," I blurt, trying to cover all bases as I drag my invitation out of my handbag, "the car brought me here and I just got out without checking." I hold out the card to her, hoping she won't snap off my arm like a furious French crocodile. "Am I at the wrong event? Is my party on another boat?"

I glance out of the porthole.

There are quite a lot of other water-bound transport options: all shining whitely as they navigate their luxurious way down the second longest river in France.

Then I peer over her shoulder into the main room of this yacht where *a* party is definitely happening.

There are lots of beautiful people, milling around

elegantly with glasses in their hands, all wearing different shades of purple.

Huh. That's very coordinated.

Although I suppose it *is* Fashion Week: they probably all discussed it beforehand by group text.

"Don't play dumb with me," the woman hisses angrily, narrowing her eyes and batting my invitation away. "You know *exactly* what you've done."

There are four hundred miles of blood vessel in the average human brain and mine feel like they're shrinking by the second.

"Um, I really don't," I admit, feeling my cheeks start to flush.

"You just *happened* to put on a dress by another designer, did you? It just *happened* to be the wrong colour and worn with neon trainers to ensure maximum press coverage? You just *happened* to prance down the purple carpet like some kind of royal fairy? *What exactly am I paying your agency thousands for?*"

I blink down at my green frock. Huh?

Paying my… *what?*

"I thought this was just a fashion party," I stammer, starting to shake again. "I wore my nicest dress especially. My best friend made it."

There's a loud crunching sound and the floor suddenly shifts slightly.

A cheer goes up from the party behind us.

The woman in front of me scowls even more deeply and looks at the ceiling.

"*Just* a fashion… For the love of… *You were supposed to wear THE PURPLE DRESS. THAT IS THE ENTIRE POINT OF YOU BEING HERE. THAT WAS YOUR JOB.*"

I open my mouth.

Oh my God: this party was one of my *actual, paid jobs?*

But where was…?

The lilac-fringed tapestry hanging over my bed. It wasn't ornamental decoration or part of the hotel's interior design decisions, was it.

That was my outfit for this evening.

A wave of embarrassment rushes over me at the exact moment that I realise I'm not only shaking with shame.

I'm literally, physically vibrating too.

My phone has been ringing on silent against my hip for the last ten minutes.

"Well, it's too late now," the designer huffs in resignation as I stare at her with round eyes. "The boat has cast off. You're stuck in *that* thing for the rest of the night." Then she turns her back on me and starts walking into the party. "Models. So *criminally* stupid."

And as I grab the phone from my handbag and see fifteen missed calls from Nat, I can't help thinking that as a broad stroke that's an incredibly unfair statement.

But in this case she has a valid point.

10

According to tests I've completed on the internet, I have got more than 143 IQ points.

I have *really* got to start spending them better.

"Harriet?" Nat blurts the second after I hit the green button and walk out on to the deck so I can look at the dark, cold river and maybe think about jumping in it. "Is that you?"

"For now," I say glumly. "I'm going to be researching scientifically unapproved body-swap options just as soon as I'm off this yacht."

"You're on a *yacht*?"

I turn the webcam on and hold my phone in the air so that Nat can witness my shame, as well as the fact that my face is now basically the same colour as the party.

The main room is bright and shiny, full of purple vinyl chairs, ostentatious lilac shaggy rugs, eye-wateringly purple drinks and huge, shiny, lilac-flower-covered mirrors. Even the snacks are garishly purple: they've got tiny muffins with violets on top.

India would basically disappear here.

"Yup, this is definitely a yacht. A fashion yacht."

I can't see many professional fishermen sailing out in this: they'd get laughed off the ocean.

"That looks *amazing*," Nat breathes as I spin the camera back to face me. "*So* swanky." Then her face twists guiltily. "Harriet, I'm sorry. You wore the wrong dress, didn't you?"

I stare at her in amazement. "How do you know that?"

"The invitation. Wilbur meant a *specific* dress, not mine," she sighs, rubbing a hand on her face. "Did you not see that expensive one hanging over your bed and the purple shoes on the windowsill? I tried to tell you, but it was waaaaay too vague given it's… well. You."

I frown.

MAKE SURE YOU WEAR THAT DRESS!

Nat didn't mean *hers* at all: she meant *Wilbur's*.

Whoops.

Also I missed the shoes *too*?

I can't believe my best friend saw what was going on more clearly than I did and she was two hundred miles away.

"Don't worry. It was inevitable that I'd do something stupid on this trip, so at least I got it out of the way early."

Nat laughs, then leans a little closer to the camera. "What have you got on your feet, H? You look three inches shorter than you should."

It's times like these that I can't believe I'm the only one in this friendship who gets A grades in physics.

Nat is clearly a spatial genius.

"Oh, I'm just, uh, squatting a bit," I lie quickly. "It's important to keep thigh muscles from atrophying... you know, while I'm posing."

Then I can feel myself start to guiltily grin.

"On the upside, it went *really* well, Nat. I mean, I got shouted at and Wilbur's going to kill me. But other than that, it went *really* well. The photographers *loved* your dress."

Her face twists as she tries to look sympathetic and beam massively all at the same time. "Really?"

"Yup. They took loads of photos. Piles. A *profusion*. And I told them it was made and designed by Nat Grey, just like we planned."

Nat whoops. "Toby's making an awesome blog for me as we speak. I love you, Harriet Manners."

"Sharpie love or just regular biro?"

"Full on face-tattoo love," Nat laughs. "And –" she glances around furtively, even though the only thing she's actually inspecting is her own bedroom – "Any sign of… *you-know-who*?"

I flinch.

In all the commotion of the past hour, I kind of forgot about the locked-up part of my brain.

"Which you-know-who?" I say cautiously.

Believe it or not, there are actually *two* boys I've been instructed to look out for in Paris this week.

One is my ex-boyfriend; the other is Nat's.

"I very much doubt that François is cycling his trusty *velo* around a Fashion Week party on a yacht," Nat says drily. "In his terrifyingly unfashionable green-Lycra shorts…"

"With his bottle of olive oil."

"Trying to give all the supermodels exfoliating foot rubs with salt he's stolen from the kitchen." Nat laughs. "Actually, who am I kidding? He's totally there. Check the galley."

I laugh. The doomed relationship of Nat and François involved a secret Italian girlfriend and did not end well.

Then I peer into the party room with a grimace.

There are so many glamorous people here, and I have no idea who any of them are. And even though it pains me to say it, I hope that none of them are Nick. Because right now I cannot cope with being trapped on a one-thousand-metre-square floating luxury prison with the boy who broke my heart.

Or whose heart I broke, for that matter.

The breaking was really kind of simultaneous.

"OK," I say, automatically holding my breath and trying to shove all thoughts of Nick back into the box in my head, "I'll report back if I see anything."

"Great," Nat nods. "And remember…"

"Pictures?"

"I was going to say *have fun*," she says, blowing a kiss. "But that too."

We wave at each other fondly, grinning.

And the phone goes dead.

I'm just mentally preparing to make my way into the Purple Party – dressed in several vivid shades of green – when there's a loud voice behind me.

"NO. WAY. *NO-SCREWBALLING-WAY.* GET OUT OF HERE!"

Eyes wide, I spin round slowly.

If the shouter means that literally, I'm going to have to swim.

"HARRIET!" screams a stunning and incredibly tall girl with black, glossy skin, pouty lips and no hair whatsoever. "As I *live and breathe.* WHAT ARE YOU DOING HERE, BABE?"

And Wilbur was right: I *do* know somebody at Paris Fashion Week.

I just didn't expect it to be *Kenderall*.

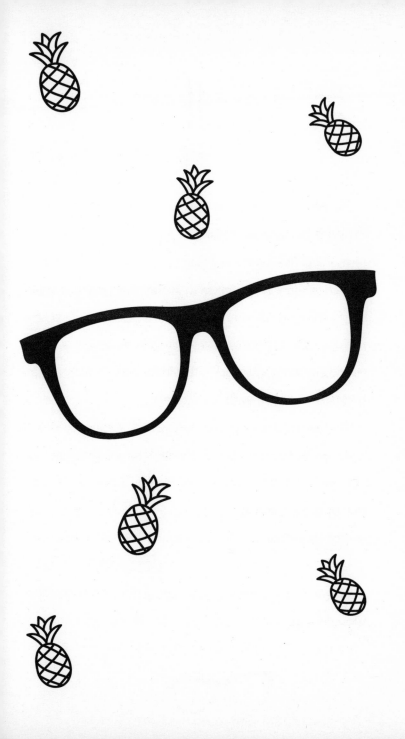

‖
—

Which is quite naive, really.

If there are over 7.4 billion people on the planet, a proportionately small amount of them are jostling about the fashion world.

So, very much like electrons in a flow of electricity, we're bound to bump into each other now and then.

At high energy, with vast impact.

And of all the people I've ever met, Kenderall – New York model-stylist, Brandist, Hyphenator and owner of a not-so-mini 'teapot' pig called Francis Bacon – must be one of the hardest to miss.

Not least because she's screaming the yacht down.

"Harriet!" she shrieks, grabbing me firmly by the shoulders as a few people turn to stare at us curiously.

"Babe, how long has it *been*? *Too long!* Like, three, four seasons?"

"S-six months," I stutter as she shakes me.

"Whoa! Well, that's what happens when you're insanely busy and successful, I guess. It's like, time just... *what's my word*?"

"Flies?"

"That's a cliché, babe," Kenderall frowns, cheekbones glittering. "Don't be a cliché. Come on, think outside the box. It's like time, *power-walks*, you know?"

My mouth twitches as a vision of a clock wiggling down the road in trainers with its little hands swinging vigorously pops into my head.

"And what have you been *doing*? You, like, vanished from New York last year. I thought you were abducted by aliens. I was *super*-concerned because that would have been the *best* publicity stunt and I totally should have done it first."

She demonstrates her latent fear for my earthbound health and safety by saying this while using an extended finger to curl her enormous eyelashes.

"Umm, I actually went back home to England, Kenderall," I explain as a few other people spin round to look at us. "Sorry I didn't let you know."

"England?" she says absently. "Oh *cute*. And it's not Kenderall any more, babe. It's Siren. Some *other* model has a name that's *really* similar and people were getting confused, even though I'm clearly better and taller so I switched it."

I blink. "*Siren?*"

"Yeah. Apparently it's some Greek goddess who was really hot. It makes me sound classy. Old-school."

"But..." How do I put this delicately? "Traditionally sirens were half women, half bird-monsters, who used to lure men to their death by singing."

And as a result it now means *loud warning noise.*

Actually, that kind of suits her.

"Cool," she says, obviously pleased. "Big fan of alluring." Then she looks me up and down. "Babe, you *finally* took my advice on board. Wearing green when everyone else is wearing purple? Nice way to be remembered."

82

I flush. Having a Kenderall-endorsed Unique Modelling Point and Self-Branding exercise was *not* the aim of this outfit. "I didn't…"

"You don't have to convince me. We're playing the same game, right? I'm just annoyed I didn't think of it first. I'm wearing the same as everyone else, like a *loser.*"

On a boat full of pretty sleek purple dresses, Kenderall (I'm just going to keep calling her Kenderall) is wearing a bright, sequined lilac catsuit with enormous orange glittery platforms that make her at least six-foot-five. So that's not *totally* accurate.

"And what happened with your model-slash-what was he again?" she adds loudly, looking over my shoulder. "You know, the boyfriend? Roughly my height, Asian, curly hair, super hot. Leaves you little boxes at parties and then disappears."

A human stomach is about the size of a fist.

Which is appropriate, because it feels like one has just entered mine: hard.

"Nick?" I manage to breathe.

"Yeah, NICK!!" She bellows at the top of her lungs.

"Are you still dating? Or did you end up driving him away after all like I told you not to?"

Weird: now it feels like my fist is about to try and enter Kenderall's stomach too.

Pain rips through my chest area.

"Uh," I manage with a dry mouth, swallowing with difficulty, "we broke up and he went back to Australia... some time ago."

Four months, twelve days and seven hours, roughly.

Not that I'm counting.

"For reals?" Kenderall frowns. "Because I could *swear* I saw him ten minutes ago. That's not a face you forget easily, babe. Although you probably know that already. Am I right?"

She holds her hand up to high-five me.

The fist in my stomach has rotated and is slowly reaching up towards my chest, preparing to punch me with a wallop there too.

The box in my head feels like it's about to explode and scatter its contents all over the bright, sparkling heart of Paris.

Nick's actually here? Nick's here. Nick's—

No. No. No. *NO.*

"I don't…" I blurt in a panic, spinning around wildly. "I can't… It's not…"

There's nothing I can do. I'm trapped on a boat sailing down the middle of the Seine.

I'm Tennyson's *The Lady of Shalott.*

Half-sick of shadows and incapable of not turning round and seeing the boy I love, I'm going to end up dying of heartbreak and entering a large body of water.

Again.

"Come on," Kenderall demands as I desperately search for a piece of furniture to crawl under. She grabs my arm and begins dragging me towards the party. "Nick's here, I'm certain of it. Let's go find him."

12

The frigate is a bird found across the majority of tropical and subtropical oceans.

It is well known for having one of the most dramatic mating calls of any species. When approaching a member of the opposite sex, the male will abruptly inflate a red, kidney-shaped sack under its throat so big it's nearly twice the entire size of the bird.

And it looks quite a lot like a beating heart.

I may not be male – or a frigate bird, for that matter – but I think I have one now too.

As Kenderall drags me bodily into the busy main room of the party, I can feel my heart getting bigger and bigger and moving up my throat until it's stuck there for the whole world to see.

Throbbing and visible like a startling red balloon.

*

"Oooh," Kenderall says, momentarily pausing by a plate of *hors d'oeuvres* and grabbing a tiny violet-topped muffin. "I really shouldn't, but I've been lifting weights this morning so my metabolism is *sky-high.*"

I open my mouth and shut it again.

Nope: still can't breathe.

I wasn't prepared for this. I suddenly feel like a human motion sensor: every single movement or sound in the room is heightened, magnified, piercing and raw.

A beautiful girl in a purple mini-dress laughs loudly to my left and I jump. A guy with a shaved head and full beard in a purple shirt takes a step to the right and every single cell in my body feels like it's been electrocuted.

A waiter taps my arm and I almost vomit on my feet.

There's a blinding flash of light.

"Look hot," Kenderall reminds me as somebody dives in front of us with a camera. She firmly grabs my waist and poses. *Flash.* "Paps *everywhere* tonight. We *are* what we *project*, babe. Fame is *within* us. We have to *be* it and *live* it."

Oh God. This is too much.

I want to get off I want to get off I want to get—

There's another flash and the designer with the blonde crop shakes her head at me from across the room.

"Well, hi there," a model with piercing grey eyes says, approaching us with his hand out. "You're Harriet, right? Wilbur has told me *so* much about—"

"*Oooh,*" Kenderall hisses, grabbing me and smacking his hand away. "Sorry, Jackson. Hold that thought."

Then she spins me around until it feels like I'm just going to keep spinning and spinning until either I collapse or the world does.

Whichever comes first.

"*There,*" she hisses, suddenly letting go. "*Told you.*"

And everything goes dark.

When I've come back to my senses – which is actually about two seconds later because all I've done is shut my eyes – there's a tall boy approaching us.

Slim and dark, with coffee-coloured skin and high cheekbones: curly hair and a wide smile.

89

He's grinning shyly at me and I don't know what to do;
I don't know what to say.

Kenderall's holding out her hand to him.

"There," she says in triumph, presenting him to me
while rubbing his arm vigorously like he's a lamp and she's
expecting a genie to pop out. "*Told you.* I so *knew* he
was here."

I may have finally stopped spinning in body but my
brain's somehow still going: spiralling on the spot with a
loud whirring sound, like a helicopter rotor.

"Hi," I say blankly.

"Hi," he says. "How are you?"

"I'm fine, thanks. You?"

"Fine, thanks."

We stare at each other, pinned to the spot.

There's no way around saying this: he's so beautiful, it's
almost unfair. It's the kind of beauty that happens so rarely
– that's such a freak anomaly of genetics – that people
will literally pay thousands of pounds to capture it for other
people to simply look at and appreciate.

I study his perfect face carefully, taking mental notes.

Eighteen months ago, I'd have blushed, stuttered, stared at the floor. Gone into some kind of embarrassed meltdown and looked for some furniture to hide beneath.

But this handsome boy could be anyone.

The canine teeth aren't pointy enough and there are no dents in his lips; there's no little duck tail at the back of his head. He doesn't smell green; there's no mole above his left eyebrow. No scar from being attacked by a seagull/rock as a little boy. I bet his eyes don't crease into crescents when he smiles and his mouth doesn't curl upwards in the corners even when he's tired.

He doesn't blink just slightly too slowly, like a calm, dark lion.

He's just a boy.

Just another really, really good-looking boy.

Because *he's not Nick*.

"*Awkward*," Kenderall says jubilantly, waggling her eyebrows at this total stranger. "God, you can *taste* the tension in the air."

The poor boy looks as bewildered as I do.

"Ah," I say slowly as both intense relief and strange

disappointment start to pulse through me, "Kenderall, I'm afraid we've never actually m—"

"*Sssssshhhh*," she interrupts, putting a perfectly manicured red-nailed finger on my lips. "Don't overtalk it, babe. Tell him how much you hate him with your *eyes.*"

I look at the stranger and he blinks back.

"*Kenderall*," I whisper into her ear as the male model looks around for an escape, standing on my tiptoes, "that's *not him. It's not Nick.*"

"It's not?" she says, spinning to stare at him. "Well, why are you still standing there, then?" She pushes the stranger away with a hand and there's a bright flash from photographers standing nearby. "Some people are just so *desperate* for attention. Now *pose,* girl."

She grabs me by the green waist and swings me towards them.

There's another flurry of lights.

And – even though I'm standing in the sparkling centre of an impromptu photo shoot – for the first time in over a week I can feel myself starting to very carefully unwind.

Nick's not here.

He was never here. He's not leaning sleepily against a lamp-post just round the corner; he's not about to appear and throw my brain into total turmoil.

My heart's not about to break all over again, in yet another foreign country.

And I don't know how to feel about it.

Finally, after a few minutes, Kenderall lets go of me, says she's hungry and wanders off to find some more bright purple muffins.

Blinking, I turn to watch the lights of Paris float by – the Eiffel Tower twinkling in blues and whites over the river, the yellow orbs of *Le Louvre* dancing in the water – and slowly the red heart in my throat stops throbbing.

It moves out of my throat.

And – little by little – it deflates until it's small enough to go back inside the box again.

13

The rest of the evening can be summarised thusly:

- Kenderall gets her new red business cards out, with *SIREN* – Model-Stylist-DJ-BeautyVlogger typed on them ("I branched out. My YouTube lipstick skills are *insane*.")

- I help her hand them out to everyone, even though they clearly don't want them

- The paparazzi continue to take photos

- I continue to take photos (for Nat)

- Every time my picture is snapped the blonde designer scowls at me

- I'm pretty sure I spot Leonardo DiCaprio.

95

Although I can't be totally sure.

He could just be a really popular blond man surrounded by lots of models and the paparazzi are discussing summer horoscopes at unnecessary volume.

By the time the party yacht docks again, it's nearly 11pm and I'm genuinely exhausted. Working into the night for demanding fashion designers is surprisingly challenging.

Even if they *are* also your best friend.

"After-party?" Kenderall says as we walk back down the gangplank together, surrounded on both sides by waiting photographers. "Chanel's is at *La Grande Galerie de l'Évolution* in *Le Muséum National d'Histoire Naturelle* and I heard Rihanna's going to be there."

I blink in surprise: Kenderall's French accent is absolutely impeccable.

Also, that sounds like *my* kind of party.

The museum has a Noah's Ark procession of taxidermy animals running right through the reception area.

"Or the after-after-party?" Kenderall continues, turning to the side and giving the photographers a quick pout. "Or the after-after-after-party?"

Grabbing her arm for balance, I can't stop a yawn escaping as there's another flash of light.

Sugar cookies.

Do they have to capture *everything*?

"I think one party a day is quite enough for me," I say sleepily, rubbing my eyes vigorously and then realising that thanks to the layers of mascara I now look like my suitcase. "I've actually got two shows to do tomorrow."

Another flash of light.

Kenderall laughs. "Babe, we've *all* got jobs tomorrow. It's Paris Fashion Week. You've just got to *live it*, you know? *Be* it. *Harness* it."

There's a sudden roar of commotion as a group of next-level beautiful girls walk down the ramp and the crowd of paparazzi erupts: screaming and shoving at each other to get to the front.

"Girls! *Les belles!* Over here!"

Kenderall glares as she gets pushed unceremoniously out of the way by a particularly enthusiastic man with a huge camera.

"Should have copyrighted my old name," she mutters darkly. "Or at least bought a trademark."

I smile, take a quick photo of the other-worldly stunning and confident models, and send it to Nat.

Then I glance at the time and start wandering towards the black Citroën waiting for me on the kerb.

I feel like I can finally focus now.

All I really want to *live*, *be* and *harness* tonight is my bed.

And maybe a unicorn, if there are options.

"Goodnight, Kenderall," I call, opening the car door. "And *thank you*."

"No problem!" she yells as the Nick-alike walks past her slightly too quickly. She winks and points at his back. "And now I'm off to PARTY with this one!"

"Go for it," I smile, clambering into the back of the car and yawning widely. "He's all yours."

I've only just staggered back into the hotel, checked briefly over the printed-out itinerary for tomorrow, thrown on my pyjamas and crept into bed when my phone starts ringing.

Which, to tell the truth, is not an enormous surprise.

I may be an international model and officially an adult in several countries around the world, but I was not given a free rein on this trip.

In fact, the conditions of my adventure have been typed on to an A4 piece of paper, underlined twice, signed and put in my suitcase: securely water-protected in a ziplock plastic bag, for good measure.

"Harriet?"

"Mmmm?" I snuggle contentedly beneath the clean white covers with my eyes shut. "Hey, Annabel."

"Are you safely at the hotel?"

"Mmmm."

"In bed?"

"Mmmm."

"Is Elle McPherson there?" I hear Dad say from somewhere nearby. "Or Liz Hurley? Did you put in a good word for me with them as promised? I ate a multivitamin today. They need to be kept aware of how healthy and strong I am for my age."

Needless to say, Dad gave me his own list to follow.

On that one I'm strictly ordered to attend every party going (including ones I may not be invited to).

"Don't worry, darling," Annabel tells him in a warm, light voice, "we'll add it to the weekly newsletter we send all the Supers."

Then she clears her throat.

"Now, Harriet. You know your father and I love you and respect you and admire you very much. Just as much as you love and respect and admire the rules we set for you. So… we'd like to see the proof of your current location, I'm afraid."

I open my mouth to object, and then realise that it wouldn't exactly be *unheard* of for me to stretch the truth with my parents. In fact, scientists have recently developed a material called *hydrogel* – a compound made of alginate, polyacrylamide and water – that can extend to twenty times its original size.

I think it's fair to say that the accuracy of what I tell my family tends to be similarly flexible.

Sighing, I switch to video-call and peer at them through one eye. "Evidence," I mumble, pointing at myself and then my crisply starched bed linen. "In bed by 11:30pm curfew, as contractually agreed."

In order to get my parents to agree to three days in Paris with only Wilbur as a chaperone, I signed up to a bedtime even earlier than Cinderella's.

"Excellent," Annabel smiles. "Tabitha says *bon nuit*, by the way. Or she would if she were conscious and capable of communication in any language."

She points her phone down at my baby sister, sleeping with Dunky, her beloved stuffed toy donkey, gripped tightly against her cheek.

A wave of love washes over me.

Also a little jealousy: I'd enjoy being asleep like that right now too.

"*Bon nuit* back," I smile through a yawn.

"Goodnight, sweetheart," Annabel says as Dad blows kisses in the background and elaborately mouths *Find Liz Hurley*. "We miss you."

"Miss you too."

And the last thing I see before I close my eyes are the people I love best in the world, smiling down at me from England.

14

Now for the science bit.

Somatotropin is a peptide hormone secreted by the anterior pituitary gland. Its purpose is to stimulate growth, cell reproduction and regeneration in animals, and it's released primarily at night: just one of the many reasons we humans need decent rest and relaxation time.

Without it, we can't repair or recover.

So when I say that – after a solid night's sleep for the first time in a week, curled up in my soft, cosy Parisian bed – I wake up feeling like a brand-new person, I don't mean that metaphorically.

My brain and heart have been healed.

I have been *literally* remade.

*

Blinking into consciousness, I roll over and smile happily in the warm winter sunshine. I pick up my phone and grin at the messages that have turned up this morning:

Hope you're kicking the fashion world's butt. Possibly literally. ;) Jasper x

Tell me nobody's wearing purple. ;) Indy x

Just discovered that Couture was actually founded by Charles Frederick Worth, WHO WAS ENGLISH. Toby Pilgrim

So it's not actually French at all. Toby Pilgrim

I think you should alert the authorities because they are definitely making it sound like it is. Toby Pilgrim

OH MY GOD LOOK AT THIS I HAVE LITERALLY NEVER BEEN THIS HAPPY THANK YOU THANK YOU Nat xOxOxOxOxOxOxOxOx

Beaming, I click on the attached image.

It's a photo of me standing on the Purple Party yacht, with Kenderall's arm round my waist, wearing the green dress: flushed and wide-eyed and smiling a tiny bit.

Underneath it says *Top models Syren and Harriet wearing Gaultier and Nat Grey at the Purple Party at Paris Couture Fashion Week.*

And it's all over the internet.

I think I'd better stay out of the way of that blonde designer or she's going to string me up from the rafters like a fluffy ginger boxing-bag.

Still, great for Nat, right?

Maybe not so great for India: she'll be furious that Paris Fashion Week has officially stolen her colour.

Smiling, I stretch wide like a cat for a few moments, then drink a large glass of water, put on my teddy slippers and pad over to the bathroom. I'm just dubiously examining the spot on my chin and trying unsuccessfully to resist the urge to squeeze it once more for posterity when there's a loud knock on my door.

"Coming!" I call, taking another gulp of water and

giving my new demonic chin-horn another tentative prod.

Then I pad back over to the door.

Wilbur bursts through it before I've even heard the door *click*: all yellow polka dots and black cape and enormous shoulder pads.

Without being rude, he looks a bit like a cheetah superhero from the eighties.

"*No*," he says, gently smacking my hand. "*Naughty.* What did I tell you about picking your spots?"

I blink at him. "I wasn't..."

"Baby, you look like you have grown your own mini volcano out of pus," he says breezily, flinging a large furry purple bag on to my unmade bed. "That's not *couture.* That's a bad Blue Peter session. But do not fret your little rabbit nose, because I'm here to save the day. Also I like today's outfit, *a propos.* It is *adorborama.*"

I stare down at my pyjama top.

It says:

What Do You Call A Dinosaur With An Extensive
Vocabulary?
A THESAURUS

The matching PJ bottoms have diplodocuses and open books drawn all over them. I had them made especially for me by a website I found on the internet to celebrate getting straight As in my GCSEs.

Nat's not the only super-cool fashion designer in my friendship group, you know.

"Wilbur," I say, gulping down another glass of hydrating, beautifying H_2O, "what are you doing here? I thought you said you'd check in by text?"

"That was *a-vent,*" Wilbur says merrily, pulling open the bag and getting pots of potions and ointments out. "Which is French for *before I got my adorable toosh kicked by my boss at Infinity at six-thirty this morning for letting you lose us another client.*"

I flush guiltily. "Oh."

"And now it is *a-pray,*" he continues, tugging out a

soft grey face-towel. "Which is French for *after I cancelled my other plans for the morning so I could make sure it didn't happen again.*"

I flush a bit harder. "Wilbur, I'm *so* sorry."

It was a genuine mistake – albeit an incredibly stupid one – and I feel awful about it. Even if my best friend did benefit rather a lot from my misunderstanding.

According to her last text, her new blog's already had 2,000 hits and only twelve of them were me.

"No need for apologiserisation, my little chocolate-chip pancake," Wilbur continues breezily. "I should have been more specific. Maybe stuck a Post-it on the wall with a neon flashing arrow pointing at THE DRESS. Maybe with the words THE DRESS written on it in neon marker pen. You know, as a special Harriet-Hint."

He carefully plucks the pale lilac dress down from the wall, whispers to it "sorry, little one" with an affectionate stroke and folds it neatly away with a tiny sigh of sadness in a special cloth-lined bag.

"But my next show isn't until lunchtime, is it?" I check,

starting to panic. "I swore it said in the itinerary I didn't need to be there until twelve-fifteen."

"That is right as a slip-stitch on two bits of adjacent fabric," Wilbur beams, putting a hairbrush on the bed.

I blink at him. "So is that correct or not?"

"It is." He gets a pair of hair-straighteners out. "Which, kitten-poodle, means we've got just enough time to get you ready."

I look at the beauty paraphernalia now piled up into heaps and almost completely covering my bed.

It looks like the only rubbish tip on the planet that Nat would pay to rummage through.

"But isn't that what stylists are for?" I say in amazement. "To make me a perfect ten?"

Wilbur laughs and looks at my throbbing chin and my fringe with toothpaste from last night still flecked at its ends.

"Monkey, they've only got so much time. I think we need to get you up to zero first."

*

An hour and a half later, my face has been properly cleaned and treated and exfoliated, my spot is miraculously almost gone, my hair is clean, soft, straight and swishy, and my eyebrows have been gently plucked into tidy, elegant arches.

And I'm now wearing green leggings and a yellow T-shirt with a cartoon of a Labrador on it. I mean, if I can't convince anyone I'm French, I may as well give up on being chic entirely.

Bouncing, Wilbur shepherds me through the hotel reception and into the black car idling by the kerb.

"Are you coming to the show?" I check as he climbs in after me. "To the first one?"

"Kitten-munch," he smiles, getting his phone out and starting to smash at it with his finger again, "for the next six hours I'm not leaving your side."

15

Now, *beauty* is obviously subjective.

The word itself comes from the Old French 14th-century term *biauté,* which means 'pretty, seductive or attractive', but we each decide what that means to us: what alignment of features or characteristics is pleasant to our own, individual senses.

However, as we all know, some places or people definitely tend to get more votes than others.

And as Wilbur and I drive through the streets of France's capital, sunlight flickering between buildings and trees, I can see why even the word itself was born here.

Beauty is in every line of Paris.

It's etched in the graceful shapes of the windows and arched doors of its houses; in the pops of blue and white

wooden shutters, the gentle greys and greens and taupes in the gradations of the stone.

It's in the weaving ivy climbing the walls and the uneven steps holding cobbled streets together; the bright blue *cafes* and little red *boulangeries,* yellow *boucheries,* pink *confiseries* or green *fromageries;* the shining windows piled high with rainbows of *macarons* and *croissants* and cheeses and cream cakes.

It's in the perfectly spaced lines of trees and organised pots of flowers, and in the size of the sky: so much bigger and more open than in Tokyo, New York or even London, mainly because very few buildings are allowed to be over five storeys high.

It's in how *regular* it is, thanks to the strict urban regulations that have kept everything in the same style for centuries. (Also because it wasn't destroyed during the Second World War and then patched up again in the sixties.)

Beauty is buried in its history and culture.

No less than a hundred and fifty-three museums;

hundreds of churches and galleries; dozens of world-class monuments including *l'Arc de Triomphe, Le Sacré-Coeur, Le Panthéon, Le Centre Pompidou*.

And in the very heart of all this light and prettiness lies *Le Louvre*: the world's biggest museum, art gallery and the old home of Napoleon, who Jasper says used to have the portrait of the Mona Lisa hanging in his bedroom.

AKA: the centre of Paris Fashion Week.

Which is why – as our car drives straight past the enormous stone façade and the huge glass and metal pyramid that serves as the museum entrance – I spin to watch it disappear behind us in total confusion.

I'm trying to find a suitably pretty way to put this.

Where the *unicorn poop* are we going?

"Umm," I say as our car crosses the river and continues into the south of the city – past the Disney-like turrets of the *Musée de Cluny* and the *Université Paris-Sorbonne* (one of the best universities in the world and on my application list for next year) – "am I not doing a catwalk show today?"

Then I swivel and watch l'*Observatoire de Paris* – one of the most important astronomical centres in the world – glide past, totally unvisited.

"You certainly are, my *petite* pot noodle," Wilbur chuckles as the car pulls to a stop in a bright patch of sunshine. "Right here, in fact."

I frown at what's propped up in the middle of the grass. "In a *tent*?"

It's rather small and white and inconspicuous, and frankly not exactly what I was expecting from the most high-fashion event this planet has to offer.

I thought there'd at least be turrets.

"*Here.*" Wilbur climbs out of the taxi and starts leading me towards the tiny marquee, grinning widely and clearly enjoying himself immensely. "On this spot *precisement*, choco-nut. Or *icy*, as the French people say."

He points at where he's standing.

I blink at the road next to us: it's full of slowly moving cars, a few statues and some pigeons. Nothing spectacular, and certainly nothing worthy of the designer royalty I thought I was about to model for.

"In the street?" I check. "Is it some kind of pop-up show? Or one of those Flash Dance type things?"

Please say no please say no please—

"Harriet Manners," Wilbur says in a disturbingly business-like voice to a woman with a clipboard standing outside the entrance. "Infinity."

"Number thirty-three," she replies after scanning her list with a quick nod.

"Baby bean-fence," Wilbur says, pausing and staring at his buzzing phone, "sorry to amend my numero-uno plan, but can you do the next few hours without me, pudding? Jessica's having a hissy-fit about the colour of her dress and the designer is going *loco*. Hand on my heartbeat, I'll *returnez* by the time it starts."

I try to smile bravely as my heart plunges. "But– but where *is* the show happening?"

As we all know, I like to be as informed as possible about everything, at all times. Not least the topography of where I'm about to walk in heels.

Wilbur beams as clipboard lady pushes open the flappy door to the marquee that has PRIVATE stamped on it in big black letters. "You will see anon, my little fish-face. In you pop."

Then he starts giggling and gently pushes me doorwards. "Ahehehehe! Or – to put more fine a point on it, kitten – *maybe you won't*. It really depends on the lighting."

I'm not sure exactly what I was expecting, but I can say with some certainty it's not this.

The marquee is flooded with brilliant light, it's boiling hot and the air is filled with a heady combination of hairspray, perfume and the faint mouldy smell that comes with temporary plastic-coated accommodation.

There are people everywhere.

Shouting, screaming, talking, occasionally singing: trying to make themselves heard over a multitude of hairdryers, all blasting and roaring away.

Models are crammed next to each other like fashionable baked beans: squished together on rickety plastic chairs with umpteen people pulling their hair in different directions, simultaneously having truckloads of make-up applied by dozens of make-up artists; standing like mannequins while pairs of stylists stitch them into dresses and glue sequins on to their collarbones.

It's hot. It's loud. It's chaotic.

And obviously I'm not an expert on these topics but it's not pretty or glamorous or sophisticated or chic *at all*.

Feeling utterly bewildered, I'm led through the artificially hot fashion-spangled mess to a seat in front of a brightly lit square mirror with '33' written on the corner in black marker pen.

To my left is an angular, brown-skinned girl with her hair in tight curlers, speaking angrily into a mobile phone held several inches in front of her face, and to my right is a curvy blonde having her lips slowly and carefully painted black.

"Yo," the blonde says somehow without moving them.

"Y-yo," I stammer, taking my seat, quickly snapping a photo of the room and sending it to Nat, then plonking my mobile on the table in front of me.

"*Parlez vous l'Anglais?*" a pretty lady with a short brown

bob says, checking the piece of paper she's holding. "You speak English?"

"Mmm," I mumble, because I'm now so overwhelmed I think I've forgotten how to.

She pops her knuckles loudly.

"Great," she says with a grin. "I'm Léonie, by the way. Let's get cracking."

16

And *get cracking* Léonie does.

For the next two hours, I am prodded, poked and rubbed so vigorously that I'm genuinely scared she's about to break me.

With a brush, she stipples and buffs my face with gossamer-thin layers of primer and white foundation until any sign of my natural complexion or spots or eyebrows have been totally obliterated.

She spreads the foundation down my neck and on to my chest, shoulders, back and down my arms: carefully daubing the paint down my fingers as if I'm some kind of modern-day geisha.

Deftly, Léonie pats me in a fine coat of white powder like she's dusting icing over a particularly large almond croissant so that I look velvety, matt and doll-like.

She holds a tissue under my lower eyelashes and begins to draw enormous circles round my eyes that slowly fade out at the edges: layering matt-black eyeshadow with sparkling black eyeshadow so that – for the second time in the last twenty-four hours – I look just like my luggage.

(Except this time a panda about to go to a disco.)

Then, with absolute precision, she begins to glue hundreds of tiny black gems round my bear eyes, spiralling outwards into spikes on my forehead and running like teardrops along my cheeks.

When I look up or down, left or right, all I can see is black glitter.

It's like living inside a terrifying kaleidoscope.

As soon as half of my face is encrusted and sparkling, Léonie gels my hair in a side parting and pins it back, and begins glueing tiny black feathers densely round my hairline and down my back.

Finally, when long black acrylic nails have been stuck on and heavy rings loaded, she applies three careful layers of jet-black lipstick.

"Nearly there," she says, carefully dabbing my bottom

lip with dark glitter. "Thanks for keeping it zipped. You wouldn't *believe* how many girls get overexcited, talk through this and ruin everything. You're so *lovely* and quiet."

I stare at my make-up artist in continued silence.

For the first time in my modelling career – possibly my life – I haven't said a single word for literally two hours. I haven't asked a single question, or made a single comment. I haven't loudly observed or analysed, quizzed or projected.

I haven't even told her that Americans spend more on beauty every year than they do on education, which is a fact I only recently found out and had planned to share immediately.

Judging by the very unfamiliar silence coming from me right now, with this brand-new gothic transformation Léonie has *literally* blown my mind.

"OK," she murmurs, taking me by the hand and passing me over to another lady with a blonde ponytail. "Your turn, Sylvie."

"Thirty-three," Sylvie nods with focus. "Thirty-three, thirty-three…" She glances up and down, then takes hold of an enormous cloth bag. "Here."

Then she turns to look at me.

There's a long pause while I wait with intense curiosity to see what's going to happen next. And also while I focus on not licking my lips: it's like playing a disappointingly low-calorie and possibly toxic version of the Sugar Doughnut Game.

Last one to ingest black glitter wins.

"Come on, sweetie," she adds slightly impatiently, shifting under the weight of the bag. "Quickly, please. We don't have time."

My eyes widen. "Time for what?" Then I stare at the World's Tiniest Piece Of Fabric, now being dragged out from behind the mirror.

OK: which one is my new outfit?

"This is your luxury changing room," she says, somehow reading my mind. "Don't worry, I'll hold it up for you while you get into the dress."

My eyes grow even rounder.

"I…" I stammer in a panic. "Is there maybe a toilet I can use or something to hide my… uh. Me?"

Léonie and Sylvie laugh. "Darling, this outfit is worth

more than the flats we live in combined. From this point on you don't leave our sight. We have bodyguards to make sure of it."

Huh. I thought the women with walkie-talkies lined soberly around the room were guarding it from outsiders: I hadn't realised they were guarding dresses from *us*.

Right. In for a penny, in for a pound.

Or a euro.

I mean, we *are* in France.

Taking a deep breath, I skip behind the little blanket, whip off my green leggings and puddle them on the floor, tear off my button-up T-shirt and try to ignore the fact that my knickers have a big rainbow drawn on the back.

With a small smile, Léonie helps Sylvie to unzip the cloth bag and pulls out an enormous dress.

Unsurprisingly, this is jet-black too.

A little more unexpectedly, it's made entirely of feathers. Huge black feathers, sewn together so perfectly I have no idea where the stitches are: it just looks like resplendent plumage, getting smaller round the waist and then larger in huge, fluffy circles until the dress hits the floor.

From the centre, the feathers point upwards into an enormous feather collar and the tips of them have been dipped in black glitter.

Believe it or not, there's actually an evolutionary reason that humans are attracted to things that sparkle: we are programmed to seek out water, and so instinctively approach things that shimmer like a river.

And it's totally working.

Without even thinking about it, I step forward and hold out my bejewelled and glitter-encrusted hands like a tiny child.

"No," Sylvie says in a voice that implies this obviously happens a lot. "No touching, please. It's *way* too precious for fingers."

Then she gently wraps the dress round me from the front and carefully starts stitching me into it. There isn't a single inch of this dress that doesn't fit snugly: it's structured and cut so perfectly that my entire body is completely encased, like a bird.

Finally, she gets another bag and pulls out a big pair of black four-foot feather wings.

I blink at them in amazement.

"They're not functional," she smiles, attaching them with a clever invisible halter to my back. "Just in case you were thinking of trying to fly away."

She sews them on to an invisible harness under my arms, and when they're secure and I'm trying not to wobble on heavy black velvet platform heels, I'm positioned back in front of the mirror so final touches can be made: a little pat of powder here, a tiny blob of glue there.

Amazed, I stare at my reflection shamelessly.

I am dark. I am fluffy and glittering. I am glorious.

I am by far the closest to a Disney villain I am ever likely to get. All I need now is a glowing green ball on a stick and a crow.

Quickly, I grab my mobile off the table, and manage to take a photo and send it to Nat despite my ridiculously claw-like false nails.

She has *got* to see this.

"But," I say as I'm led into a line of similarly ornamented girls, turning rigidly to look at the rest of the room, "I still don't understand. Where are we doing the show?" Last time I looked, there was nothing outside except frozen snowdrops, desultory pigeons and a stream of grey cars.

Almost everybody is ready.

Roughly fifty female models, in various styles of black gown. A tall, curvy brunette is wearing shiny, tight black rubber with large, sequined horns spiralling out of the top of her head. A beautiful, dark-skinned girl next to her is in thick, heavy black lace that stops at her shins with black wires stretching out from underneath it to the floor.

In the corner, a stunning blonde in a filmy, chiffon-layered black dress and huge black knickers is having a strand of her white-blonde hair re-curled above her jewel-encrusted face.

Thank *goodness* I didn't get that outfit.

Annabel would have sued everybody in the room.

"We *are* showing here, in fact you're standing right on top of your catwalk, but –" Léonie smiles as the tent door opens in a flash of fresh air and we are led outside in a long black, glittering and freaky line – "only in the most *literal* sense."

*

Confused, I blink in the winter sunshine as I'm practically blinded by the dazzle of my face jewels.

There's no traffic near us any more and running across the road outside are thick black carpets where no black carpets were before: lined with giant cut-glass black vases full of towering roses, sprayed black.

There are dozens of intricate black origami birds hanging from the lamp-posts, and spirals of dyed-black ivy curling down them. Lit candles in ornate black lanterns are lined along the carpet – glittering even in the sunshine – and positioned in a neat formation are men and women wearing crisp black suits, keeping at bay the passers-by now accumulating curiously at the edges.

Black swathes of chiffon drift in the wind from the trees and black carvings of demons sit amongst them, poking out like naughty little sparrows.

And in the middle, sober in the bright sunlight, is an intricately carved and Gothic-looking black gateway, above which hangs a sign:

ENTRÉE
DES
CATACOMBS

Apparently there are a number of doorways to hell spread around the world. There's *Fengdu* in China, and *Hellam Township* in Pennsylvania; the burning gases of *Derweze* in the Karakum Desert and *Murgo* in India.

There's even the official Gates of Hell, cast in bronze a hundred years ago by Rodin.

But I think we can now add this one to the list.

With its curving, ancient-looking gables, it's one of the creepiest things I've ever seen.

And as I look down at my black-velvet-encased feet, it feels as if I've suddenly developed X-ray vision and can see straight through the soil to the bones resting seventy-five feet below.

I finally understand what everyone has been talking about.

17

The Paris of today is all beauty and sunshine.

But running directly beneath it – under the feet of 2.24 million Parisians – are two hundred kilometres of narrow, deep, dark tunnels called *Les Catacombs De Paris*.

A lot of tourists don't even know they're there.

They visit the capital of France in their millions every year without realising that in the late 1700s Paris ran out of places to put their dead people and had to come up with a new solution.

So – little by little, with eerie, overnight, candlelit processions – the Parisians of 1774 began digging up graves: exhuming corpses and carrying them to abandoned quarries underground.

And slowly but surely they lined these tunnels with the remains of six million dead people: building walls

from their bones and skulls, depositing most of their passed-away Parisians and a few tourists down here for all eternity.

Which is kind of ironic, really.

Because it means that directly beneath the City of Light – wherever you are – lies a City of Darkness.

The sunny side of Paris is always up.

Trying not to scratch at the beads stuck to my face, I look down the road, to exactly where Wilbur had been pointing when he left me outside the tent. *You'll see. Or maybe you won't, it depends what the lighting is like.*

Huh.

I knew the *Catacombs of Paris* existed, obviously, but I missed three important clues:

a) I had no idea where the entrance to the tunnels was

b) I never thought anyone would hold a fashion show underground

c) *I didn't know the remains of dead humans could be hired out for recreational purposes.*

A bolt of excitement rushes through me.

Ooh, apparently there's a heart made out of human skulls lining one of the walls: if there's time afterwards maybe I can go and look for it.

I can take a photo for Nat: she'd like that.

There are also French Revolution scratchings on the wall that India would enjoy and a constant 55-degree-Fahrenheit temperature that I could measure for Toby with an app on my phone as long as we're down there long enough.

In fact, this was actually on my list of Things To Do In Paris anyway.

I can feel myself getting increasingly hyper again.

If there's one thing I *love*, it's multitasking.

The girls both behind and in front of me, however, are apparently not so sure.

Nervous tension is rising by the second.

"*Ah non,*" the beautiful brown-haired girl in black

sequins murmurs nervously as the line that looks like a glamorous death march starts to disappear anxiously through the gates. "*Non non non. Qu'est-ce que c'est*?"

I turn round as carefully as I can, trying not to knock her off her stilettoed feet with my gargantuan wings. "It's officially the biggest mass grave on the planet," I explain patiently. "Although it was also used as a Nazi bunker during the war so it's quite multipurpose. I guess all the death and ghosts and maybe poltergeists made it feel appropriate."

Her dark-painted eyes widen in terror.

"Don't worry," I add as reassuringly as I can, "nobody has died in there for *ages.*" I pause. "There *was* a man called Philibert Aspairt who got lost in 1793 and his body was only found eleven years later, right by an exit, but I'm sure there's proper signposting now."

Her shallow breathing in her tight, corseted dress gets even swifter. "I know *what* it is," she says in a heavy accent, "I mean *why* are we going in?"

OK, honestly that's a *lot* less easy to answer.

"Fashion?" I guess with an uneasy shrug.

Silently, the glittering, jittering black line continues shuffling forward until I'm on the black carpet outside the portal. The darkness gapes in front of us like something from a Bram Stoker novel, and the heads of the girls in front of us are slowly melting into the gloom like nightmarish shadows.

"*Zut alors*," sequin girl behind me breathes. "*Je ne l'aime pas.*"

Now obviously, I'm not the kind of person who believes in ghouls or afterlives or the continued adventures of the dead and decomposing.

Not only are any of the above scientifically unproven, but approximately a hundred and eight billion people have died in the history of mankind: there just wouldn't be enough space for all of us to keep hanging around.

But still.

Something deep inside me clearly isn't quite so sensible, because I'm starting to feel tiny chills all over. Up and down my spine, like the gentle, furtive tips of icy cold fingers.

Or – you know.

An analogy less sentimental. Like when you look down and realise an earwig has been climbing up your arm for the last six minutes and you didn't even see it.

Casting around, I take in one final, longing gaze at the daytime sunshine: at a city literally built on light.

Then with my head lowered, I bend down as far as my feathered bodice allows.

And move into the night.

18

Or I try to, anyway.

As everybody knows, I don't tend to have the strongest sense of spatial awareness at the best of times, and that's when I *don't* have four-foot wings stapled to my back.

With a loud *ooo-ooomph*, I manage to hit the edges of the gateway on both sides.

Then – with a slightly less loud *ooomph* – the French model behind me slams into my spine.

"*Pardon*," she murmurs.

"*Ow*," the girl behind her complains angrily after another thud as somebody rams into her too. "Get your heel off the train of my dress."

"What's going on up there?"

"Bad Angel's stuck in the doorway to hell."

There's a ripple of relieved laughter suddenly breaking

the serious atmosphere and a hot flush of embarrassment washes over me.

Get it together, Harriet.

You are here to model for a world-famous designer, not provide comic relief like some kind of Shakespearean fool.

Flushing, I mumble *pardonez-moi* down the line and twist slightly so I can enter sideways, like a glamorous feathery crab. There's a long, deep and curving iron staircase: perilously narrow and uneven, with a queue of totally silent girls disappearing carefully down it. The bottom is pitch-black and each step looks like it can barely hold the weight of one girl, let alone fifty.

Plus they've doubled my width: somebody didn't think this through properly.

Or they did but they've never met *me*.

Squinting, I suck my breath in and try to make myself as narrow and sylph-like as possible.

I focus on hanging on to the railing with my hands as hard as I can so I don't slip down them.

And I keep scuttling forward.

*

The darkness is overwhelming.

As soon as the sunshine disappears, the tunnel walls close in around us and the blackness spreads uncontrollably, like the ink of every lidless pen I've ever left in my bag, ever.

With focus, we all make our way with infinite slowness down the spiral staircase and into the narrow corridors at the bottom.

The air is thick and stale, and it's so silent now I can hear the steady breathing of the other models, the taps of their heels and the tips of my wings making *swoosh* sounds against the exposed, cold, damp grey bricks.

Every ten or fifteen steps there's a small yellow light, and as we walk in and out of dark spots the shadows of our bizarre outfits flicker and stretch around us like nightmares.

Or maybe like a particularly tall and skinny cast of *Where The Wild Things Are.*

But we all keep shuffling on.

Shivering and focused, through tunnel after tunnel, down and further down: twisting to the left and to the right and to the left again until I'm starting to feel a lot of sympathy for Philibert because I now have no idea where we are or – much more importantly – how to get back out again.

Past creepy little enclaves blocked by iron bars.

Over cold, crunchy ground.

Now and then, somebody will whisper "What was that?" or "Did you just touch me?" or "If I get bone dust on this dress my agent will *kill* me."

But mainly we're totally silent.

Overwhelmed by where we are, and what we're about to do.

Finally, we reach an opening.

It's a large cave, shaped roughly out of stone to the right of our tunnel. There's a black velvet curtain hanging in front of it and all the models are carefully ducking round and collecting there like one half of a Gothic chess set: glittering in the strange light.

A clapping sound echoes in the chamber and we all spin towards it.

"*Right, girls,*" a lady in a strange, puffed-up orange dress shouts in an English accent, her voice muffled by the thick underground air. "We couldn't brief you above ground as we had to get you down here before the audience starts arriving."

Everyone nods obediently, anxious to impress.

The French girl behind me smiles nervously, so I smile back in comradeship.

I'm glad I have a friend down here, just in case I was wrong about the whole ghost thing.

"This," the lady continues, "is going to be *the* highlight of Paris Couture Week. The eyes of the world are on us, every big newspaper will be covering it and the most major fashion players on the planet will be in attendance, so please listen to the following instructions carefully."

There now isn't a sound in the chamber.

I'm pretty sure fifty girls are holding their breath simultaneously: too terrified now to even respire.

"You all have numbers," she continues. "Once the audience is positioned and the music starts, you will walk, precisely fifteen seconds after the girl in front of you."

There's an abrupt *"ah ah AH CHOOO"* and the lady freezes while the muscles in her neck tighten like wires.

"Sorry," the model who just sneezed whispers in shame. "Dust."

Then there's a sharp, disgusted silence while we all sympathetically pray our basic body functions take the hint and stop completely.

"At some point along the tunnel," the creative director continues, "you will find an enclave with your number. When you reach it, stop. Choose a position and stay as still as possible. When the bell rings, change position. And so on until the end. Is that clear?"

There's another silence.

"Is that *clear*?" she barks again.

We all break into fervent nods and the room is suddenly filled with a cacophony of terrified whispers: *"yes" "oui" "da" "si" "yah" "hai" "diakh" "shi" "ja" "haan" "hanji" "ano" "evet"*.

I blink in amazement: just how many different nationalities from all over the world are crammed into one tiny space?

Ooh: maybe while we wait I can find out.

"Good," the creative director says sharply. "I'll only tell you once."

A badly placed light from the wall is hitting just under her chin and up her slightly round orange dress, unfortunately transforming her into a glamorous glowing Halloween pumpkin. "We have twenty-six minutes until the show starts and the only way to access it is via this corridor. To maintain an illusion of drama, I don't want to hear a single sound from any of you."

I glance around at all my potential friends.

Ah, *sugar cookies.*

What a wasted opportunity.

"Ah-ah-ah-*CHOO,*" the girl sneezes again. We all turn round. "I'm *sorry,*" she whimpers again. "*I think I'm allergic to dead people.*"

Then we turn back to the creative director.

"We are about to make history," she says, folding her arms tightly. "Starting right *now.*"

19

A lot can happen in twenty-six minutes.

In twenty-six minutes, one and a half thousand planes will take off around the world.

In less than half an hour, nearly seven hundred people will get married, six and a half thousand babies will be born and 2,782 people will die. Three billion packages will be sent and Oprah Winfrey will make $14,000 dollars.

More than seven billion hearts will beat, two thousand times each, and fourteen billion lungs will breathe.

And under the pavements of Paris, standing in the dark and cold, fifty young models from around the world are currently doing none of those things.

I'm pretty sure even our blood has stopped pumping.

That's how terrified of screwing this up we all are.

*

Time feels like it's stopped.

As we shift from leg to leg *en masse*, trying to stay comfortable in our extraordinary outfits without making a sound, it's hard not to think about the six million people around us who no longer hop, or breathe, or sneeze: who used to shake and worry and dream like us, but are now lying in the dark.

And I can't help wondering, if spirits actually exist, what 18th-century Parisians would think of how fifty lucky and privileged girls are currently spending our Saturday afternoon.

Clad in satin and lace and elaborate head-pieces and bows and beads, staying as quiet as possible.

Actually, given what I've read about the French Revolution, they're probably quite empathetic.

They may have seen it before.

Finally, there's a loud chime.

From the walls, a deep, slow beat reverberates and the sound of an organ begins to wind around it: ascending and descending slowly, like a creepy spider. The air is filled with discordant singing voices and piano and violins, then a startlingly plinky xylophone and a faint wolf howling, even though there haven't been wolves in Paris for many hundreds of years thanks to deforestation.

Quietly, a man wearing a razor-sharp black suit makes sure we're all in numerical order and gives the girl at the front a nod.

"*Allez*," he says, opening the curtain.

She swishes out and he starts counting backwards from fifteen in French.

"*Allez*," he says again.

Another confident, composed swish.

Fifteen seconds later: "*Allez*."

"*Allez*."

"*Allez*."

"*Allez*."

And as the line gets shorter and shorter, I can feel my heart start to pound and my hands quiver, the cold shivering down my back in icy trickles.

"*Allez*."

"*Allez*."

"*Allez.*"

Breathing hard, I lift my chin.

"*Allez.*"

With my eyes shut, I hold my shoulders back and try to focus on my centre of gravity: from what I've measured, it's somewhere just below my belly button. *I am a mysterious spectre. A phantom of constructed femininity, a shadowy bird-woman siren.*

"*Quinze, quatorze, treize, douze, onze, dix, neuf, huit, sept, six, cinq –*"

Bracing myself, I open my eyes again.

"*Quatre, trois, deux.*"

I take one last breath.

"*Un.*"

And – like a monstrous vision of the night – I plunge into the catacomb.

20

There's a first time for everything.

And I think clomping stridently through a dank giant underground crypt to the sounds of wolves howling while wearing a gown of glossy black feathers and a pair of freaking *wings* is definitely one of them.

Swaying and swishing and trying not to wobble off my velvet platform heels, I move through the dark.

Just ahead, I can see the trailing black ruffled skirt of the girl in front of me, brushing along the stone floor, and behind me I can hear my new French friend clipping along in her even more enormous heels.

Keep walking, Harriet.

The walls are starting to widen now.

As the music begins to get louder, screaming and wailing, we walk and twist round dark corners and the ceiling starts to lift: opening up until we're in what looks like an underground chapel. Stone arches rise above us and in the dips of grey walls are hundreds of flickering candles. Shadows quiver, the air thickens and simultaneously gets colder, and white crosses are wedged aggressively into the corners.

Condensation drips gently on to the floor.

Crouched against the walls like silent spiders are dozens of black-clothed photographers with enormous cameras, waiting for us quietly: clicking and flashing as we glide by.

Along the sides are black chairs, neatly lined up like a sartorial funeral.

In them are dozens of important men and women, glossy in expensive shades of white and ivory, fur and lace: the royalty of the fashion world. Leaning forward in total silence, holding notepads, watching us intently.

And above us, carved in rock, it says:

ARRÊTEZ
C'EST ICI L'EMPIRE DE LA MORT

Unless I really shouldn't have got a B for Year 9 French that means:

STOP.

This Is The Empire Of The Dead.

And it seems like good advice – not to mention a pretty territorial attitude from the afterlife – so it takes every single bit of willpower I have not to obediently draw to a halt and then retreat in open terror.

Instead, I keep walking.

Down past the lines of people, round another corner and an even larger, hollowed-out chamber edged with yet more beautifully dressed people sitting in chairs, lit by candles.

Except this time the walls are no longer made of stone: they're bobbly and bumpy and greyer, composed of differently sized pieces, cemented together.

Some of them are tiny, the size of the end of my finger, and some of them are larger, the size of my upper leg. Scattered throughout them in neat and coordinated patterns – as if somebody centuries ago was playing a weird game of Tetris – are rounder bits with huge black holes in them.

And as I swish straight through – trying to focus directly ahead of me through my candelit, glittery tunnel vision – a thrill runs across my shoulders, neck and the back of my head.

They're bones.

Thousands and thousands and thousands of bones.

Femurs and metacarpals; phalanges and humeri; shoulder blades and collarbones. All glued together to form the walls.

I am literally walking past the exposed craniums and gaping eye sockets of hundreds of dead people.

And all of a sudden my urge to wander off into the dark on my own or measure the temperature of the catacombs on my iPhone app isn't quite as fervent any more.

Maybe I'll leave that for another visit.

Shaking, I walk on.

Round yet more corners: past yet more stylish, perfectly groomed people in white.

The organ chimes; the wolf howls; the xylophone plinks; the drums pound.

The discordant music swells to a creepy crescendo.

And – just as it feels like I'm going to be walking in the dark forever, and I can't work out whether this is the entrance to hell or we're now definitely inside it – the model in front of me turns a corner and disappears completely.

Teetering on my heels, I almost slam to a stop.

Then I look to the side: in an enclave lined with yet more bone-walls, the number '33' has been drawn on the floor in chalk.

Abruptly, I turn into it.

Panicking, I put one hand on my hip, bend my shoulder forward at an extreme angle, curve my neck back and my head up.

I freeze like a statue.

And realise – with a sudden pang of horror – that I think I might need the toilet.

21

Here are some facts I'm thinking about right now:

1. The average human bladder holds between 300ml and 600ml of urine, which is roughly a can or two of fizzy drink
2. It can stretch to about six inches in length
3. Most people pee on average seven times a day
4. I have only been once this morning
5. That was a mistake.

I'm trying to focus, really I am.

But – slowly and surely – my body is beginning to take over from my brain: as it always does in times of emergency.

Gradually, my attention is shifting from bone categorisation and awareness that I'm part of such an

incredible, once-in-a-lifetime sartorial experience, to the terrifying sensation that my bladder might be about to explode everywhere like one of the water balloons Alexa threw at me in Year 9.

Never mind dead people: every muscle in my very-living body is starting to burn, my tummy is spasming, my shoulder hurts, my spine aches.

Insects don't have bladders because they never need to pee, and honestly I've never wanted to be a beetle more in my entire life.

I think this pose I've struck was definitely another error.

Ding.

With the loud chime, I swiftly swing my neck in the other direction, push out my other hip, hold a hand in the air and face the other way: exactly as the famous Venus de Milo statue would have done before her arms fell off.

Then I hold this pose as carefully as I can.

All of the other models must have found their places now, because slowly the audience is starting to leave their seats and walk past: photographers begin to appear in front of me, wielding their cameras like enormous weapons.

Click click click. Flash.

Ding.

Panicking, I try to think of another position that will give my bladder a break.

Twisting round, I look upwards and hold both my arms above my head like a Degas ballet dancer in the gloomy half-light, trying to keep my face as vacant and enigmatic as possible.

"I like this *very* much," a woman in a white dress says, peering at me over the top of her glasses critically. "It's atmospheric. A bit *je ne sais pas.* This girl genuinely looks scared."

I *am*, just not for the reason she thinks.

And I *do* know why: I might be about to pee myself in a couture dress that is worth more than twenty-two years of university fees or my family home.

An eternity passes, then:

Ding.

Shifting, I crouch over and turn slightly so that my wings

are more on display and my face is cast in shadow. In the process squishing my stomach and causing even more pain. *Ouch.*

Eventually the ladies move on and another set pass with murmurs of approval, making notes in their little pads.

Click flash *click.*

Ding.

"That dress is *magnificent*," somebody says as – in a moment of brain-blank and excruciating relief as I move again – I straighten with my legs in a Y shape and stupidly put my fists on my hips as if I'm Superman.

Haute Couture, Harriet. HC.

Not DC.

"I love how the structural shapes of these dresses have an innocence to them," a man in a white shirt and pale grey trousers says as a woman gets two centimetres away from me and goes "*mmm, mmmm*". Right. In. My. Face.

"There's a real *luminosity* to the collection."

"I agree. Dark but also light, simultaneously."

"Eerie but relatable."

"Absolutely. True genius."

Ding.

And in my self-induced pain I can feel my mind starting to separate from my body: floating a couple of metres above my shoulders like a hot-air balloon. What are the other models doing in their separate enclaves? What kind of shapes are they pulling?

Is there a public portaloo down here and will anyone notice if I slip into it, leaving my wings hanging on the wall outside?

Can I just squat behind a wall of bones?

What happens to your eternal soul if you accidentally pee on dead bodies?

Ding.

Pressure unbearable, I cross one leg in front of the other and squeeze them together tightly.

That's better.

Then I close my eyes. *Come on, Harriet. Get through it. Hold on just a little longer. You are the master of your fate, the captain of your… undercarriage.*

Click click click. Flash.

Ding.

Shifting again, I keep my legs crossed and straighten, putting an awkward hand on my own shoulder. This feels like the worst game of Musical Statues *ever*.

Ding.

Finally – when I can hardly bear it any longer – I lift my head, cross my legs the other way, put my claw-like hands into a *Vogue* box shape round my face and open my eyes.

And nearly lose the game completely.

Because standing directly in front of me, dark dress sucking the candlelight out of the room, magenta lipstick gleaming and eyes narrowed – like the world's most fashionable arachnid – is the only person on this planet who could make me pee myself *without* a full bladder.

The most terrifying woman or human or mammal I've ever met in my life.

And one I definitely thought I'd never see again.

Yuka Ito.

22
_

Ah, *sugar cookies.*

23
—

Seriously: *sugar cookies from hell.*

24

ALL the nightmare sugar cookies.

25

With little icing horns and forked tails.

26

Apparently if you're over forty-five years old, the world's population has doubled in your lifetime.

Which is good to know.

Because without counting, I can tell you for a fact there'll be about three hundred trillion people roaming the earth by the time this moment is finally over.

Minute after minute ticks by in silence.

Unable to even blink, I continue to hold watery eye contact and Yuka continues to stare at me. Face mask-like and stony; thin body straight. Long black lace dress immaculate as always. Little sideways pillbox hat, perched on top of her long, black glossy hair as if somebody just hit her with a miniature black omelette.

She might be one of the world's biggest fashion designers

173

– and the woman who gave me my first big break – but Yuka Ito has obviously eschewed the dress code and is actually permanently styled as if she should be modelling in this show or possibly part of this crypt, not watching it.

And she knows.

She *knows*.

I don't know *how* she knows, but she does.

Somehow – with one cold, Narnia-like stare – Yuka Ito is peering into the middle of my heart and body and she knows that I desperately need the toilet.

Probably because these are similar to the positions I pulled when I was trying to secretly study for a physics exam while advertising her perfume.

Inexplicably, she always sees straight through my subtle modelling tricks.

Motionless, I stare back.

The music continues to soar, the wolves continue to howl: my skin is starting to crawl with fear. Forget the bones; forget the skulls; forget the tomb of six million rotting skeletons. This is by far the most scared I've been since I got down here.

I hear a sneeze echo down the tunnel and pray fervently that I'm not allergic to dead bodies too. Cold sweat is starting to prickle on my throat and between my shoulder blades.

And all I can think of is the last time I saw Yuka – when she brutally fired me in Tokyo – and the last contact we had: when I quite rudely refused to take my job back, by email.

And how much she looks like her nephew.

Who she's probably seen recently.

But will definitely – without a shadow of a doubt – tell *all* about this, probably over a hearty family breakfast in the near future.

The seconds tick by, clunk by clunk.

Time stretches out eternally like a hot elastic band.

Finally – just when I can't hold any of it any more – there's a *ding*. In a move of sheer desperation, I lift my taloned hands and hold them firmly in front of my panda eyes so I can't see a single thing.

And when I take them away again, the space is empty. Yuka has gone.

27

You see?

This is what happens when you let your guard down and relax too much: you take your eye off the ball and someone kicks it straight into your face.

There are six million dead bodies down here already.

From the ice-cold expression on Yuka's face, I think I just narrowly avoided becoming another one.

Still shaking so hard I must look like a giant raven in a bird bath, I manage to change position as enigmatically as possible another four times while wishing I had the internal water-holding capacity of an elephant, instead of a field mouse.

"You know, I think she's one of my favourites," a blonde woman in a white lace top and white trousers says, again

inches away from my face. "I feel like she's really giving this show an additional level of *emotion*."

"*Absolutely*," her assistant agrees, scribbling notes on a pad. "Just look at the *concentration* on her face."

"Although I think she might be slightly too short for my show. Write that down too."

"Too short," the assistant murmurs, nodding.

As if I'm not standing directly in front of them, capable of understanding this entire conversation.

Gradually, the crowds start to thin out until all I can see is the gloomy bone-lined tunnel stretching away from my enclave on either side.

Finally there's another loud clapping sound.

"OK, girls!" the creative director calls, her voice bouncing through the tunnels. "Good job! That went perfectly! You can all start making your way—"

I don't wait to hear anything else.

Within milliseconds, I'm waddling urgently and crabbily in my priceless gown back down the passage: into the darkness again, squidging past the seventeen models standing between me and the exit.

"Excuse me," I say, shuffling against the wall and trying not to snag my trailing wingtips on bricks or bones or nose cavities. "Sorry. *Pardonez-moi. Excusez-moi.* Sorry sorry sorry. Excuse me, please. *S'il vous plaît.*"

Disorientated, I scuttle through the darkness and burst sideways into the light, blinking as my face jewels kaleidoscope spangles of sunshine around me. Trying to look aloof, I scoot past the photographers waiting on the outside for any ad-hoc opportunities.

"I have another job to get to," I blurt out, waddling past like a posh penguin. "It's… uh… very important and glamorous and urgent and totally fashion-related."

They take a few snaps that I fervently hope don't make it on to the internet.

Then I hurl myself into the backstage tent.

"Out," I whimper, grabbing wide-eyed Sylvie and Léonie. "Out out out. Please help me out of this dress."

Nodding, they quickly unstitch and un-wing me.

"Well, at least the dress survived," Sylvie says as I pull a random giant T-shirt over my head and leg it to the separate tiny tent outside.

Oh God oh God oh God –

Thank you thank you thank you thank you.

Because I think it's fair to say I've learnt a lot of things about fashion in the last fourteen months. I've learnt that the first pair of Doc Martens was made from old tyres, and denim has existed for 7,000 years.

I've learnt that Mark Twain – author of *Huckleberry Finn* – invented and patented the bra-clasp, and the Quakers had a "modesty tunnel" so that they could get across the beach in their swimsuits without being seen.

I've even learnt that in the 18th century toddlers wore high heels and probably still walked more elegantly in them than I do.

But of all the things I've learnt, *have a wee before a fashion show* is right at the top of the list and now committed by the fires of the underworld to my long-term memory.

It's definitely not a lesson I'll need to learn again.

28

I recover surprisingly quickly.

By the time Wilbur has turned up, thirty minutes later, I'm back in my normal clothes with a clean face, no feathers or jewels attached anywhere to my person and with a strong desire to never drink water again.

"Hello, wombat," my agent grins as I grab my bag, say goodbye to the French model (her name is Camille) and Sneezy Girl (an American called Joy) and leave the backstage tent. "I saw you, bunny-button! You were a thing of *wonder*, my little artfully frayed jumper."

Huh. Maybe I *did* get away with it, after all.

"But I didn't see you," I beam in pleased confusion. "Were you down there too?"

"That's probably because you had your paws across your face like the kitten I have on a fridge magnet," Wilbur

giggles. "It was like you were playing hide-and-seek, muffin, and I didn't want to spoil the fun in case you found yourself."

Ah.

OK: that wasn't one of my strongest ever poses.

"So what's next?" I say, glancing in anticipation around at the sunny street. The black carpets are already being rolled away: fashion waits for no man or woman, apparently. "I've got another show now, right?"

There's a silence while Wilbur stares at his phone.

"Right?" I say again.

Another silence.

"Wilbur?" I prompt, nudging him. "Hello?"

He blinks upwards. "Hello? We did that bit already, didn't we?"

Then his mobile buzzes again and he frowns at it.

"Are you OK?" I say as he scrolls through another message. "Has something happened?"

Wilbur shakes his head, then nods.

"Jocasta has twisted her ankle," he says quickly, bashing

at the screen again. "She can't walk, Versace starts in eighteen minutes, and I'm trying to get hold of Kiko in the neighbouring marquee but she is almost definitely snoggalogging with her boyfriend and won't answer."

I screw my nose up.

Snoggalogging is not a real word and I won't be sending it off to the Oxford English Dictionary committee at any point in the near future either.

They've already got fifteen of my applications.

"Wilbur," I say as he holds the phone up to his face, "you need to go. If you leave now you can find Kiko in person."

He studies my face. "May non, dandelion-breath. I pledged to stay with you and I've already had one little detour."

But he looks really anxious.

I've already lost him one client this week: I can't be responsible for another.

Maybe I can kind of make up for it now.

"*Go*," I say, pushing him with my hand and summoning up all my positive vibes. "Wilbur, I can do this. You sent me all of the details this morning and I am *really* good at following a comprehensive itinerary. It's kind of a natural life skill. Trust me."

He doesn't look like he trusts me in the slightest.

I don't screw up *that* frequently, do I?

"But –" he objects, looking around the street at the other models climbing into their pre-booked taxis – "all the cars are already taken, possum. By the time I've got on the Métro…"

"Then take our car," I interrupt, pointing at the familiar black Citroën waiting for us on the kerb. "My next show isn't for –" I glance at my watch – "two hours and twelve minutes. I've got *plenty* of time to get to the *Molitor*."

There may even be time to pop into the Monet Museum, which is basically next door, and pick a postcard of blobby lilies for Jasper: he really likes them.

Wilbur wavers for a few seconds.

"Baby monkey-face," he says dubiously, "you are the light bulb in my lamp and whatnot, but we all know what normally happens when you are left to your own devices. It's like leaving a lamb made of ice cream out in the sun."

Ouch.

"Don't be silly!" I laugh, guiding him gently towards the car. "I've been to Paris *plenty* of times before and I know my way around. I'll be *fine.*"

He pauses again. "Are you sure?"

Grinning, I pull a huge and well-prepared map out of my satchel and open it up. "Wilbur, I don't want to blow my own trumpet, but I am an *expert* orienteer. I got my Orienteering Guide badge *twice*. I *led* the Year 7 Geography trip. I officially know my way around a city."

I also got my Out And About Brownie badge, but nobody seems to take that as seriously. Maybe because you need a responsible adult with you at all times.

Also, it's primrose yellow. That doesn't help.

"If you're *certainment*," Wilbur says, taking another tentative step towards the taxi. "Because if I swoop in like Batman for Versace they might give me another free handbag. And they *are* fabulous and make me look *scrummy*."

"Go," I smile affectionately.

I mean, I've been underground already once today: one

more time can't hurt. At least this time there should be ninety-nine per cent fewer bones around me and they'll hopefully be supporting living bodies.

Plus, I've already screwed up twice in the last twenty-four hours.

And I know my statistics.

What's the chance of me screwing up again?

29

Here are some interesting facts about the French underground:

- The word 'metro' is used in fifty-five different countries, and comes from the Paris Métropolitain
- It travels 600,000 miles a day, which is the equivalent of ten times around the earth
- Every building in Paris is within 500 metres of a station
- I know exactly how to ride it.

I've successfully navigated Moscow, New York, Tokyo, Marrakech, London and a field in Surrey three years ago. This should be a *doddle*.

According to my map, *Denfert-Rochereau métro* station

is the closest to the Catacombs gateway, and sure enough: as I wave Wilbur off and watch him disappear down the road towards *Le Louvre*, I can see it looming straight ahead of me.

Grinning, I bounce over to the entrance.

Feeling a little bit smug, I hop down the stone stairs under the pretty, intricately carved sign arching over my head and into the small station.

I buy my ticket with a triumphant "*un* ticket *s'il vous plaît*" and decide that maybe Year 9 French is all you really need anyway.

Then I bob over to the Métro map.

According to my print-out I need to get to *Porte d'Auteuil,* which is on line ten somewhere, and then I'm basically done.

Target Independent Fashion Model: achieved.

Smiling, I wait patiently while tourists with not as many orienteering guide badges as me stand in front of the Métro map for ages.

Then I make my way to the front.

Porte d'Auteuil. Porte d'Auteuil…

Huh.

This isn't exactly what I was expecting.

The Paris Métro map doesn't look like any underground train system I've ever seen before. (And I've studied quite a few – even if I've no current plans to visit the cities they're in. You cannot be too prepared when it comes to maps.)

There are about a billion different stations scattered over an entire rainbow of randomly wiggly lines: pink, light green, dark green, yellow, mustard, light blue, dark blue. All diving and weaving in and out of each other in a chaotic tapestry, as if somebody just snatched up the London Underground and, like a ball of multicoloured string, dropped it from a great height and now it's rolled everywhere.

Blinking, I get a bit closer.

OK, maybe I just need to work out where I am now first. Figure out my strategy moving forward from that point on, rationally.

Denfert Rochereau. Denfert Rochereau…

Scanning the hundreds of tiny words, I have no idea

where the station I'm in is either. There isn't even a little sticker that says YOU ARE HERE in any language whatsoever.

Frowning, I thrust my nose forward until I'm about two inches from the map. It's all *Saint* and *Sevres* and *Alma* and *Porte* and words I don't understand.

So I step back to take in the overall picture.

Now it just looks like brightly cooked spaghetti, recently thrown against the wall.

Second by second, I can feel alarm starting to pulse through me.

What is wrong with the French Métro system?

Swallowing, I grab my phone, connect to the internet, find the Paris Route Planner and plug in where I am and where I want to go.

Then I stare at the results.

There's a green, and a six, and a mustard, and a ten.

Charles de Gaulle-étoile and *Boulogne Pont de Saint-Cloud* are involved somehow too, but nobody is really explaining why or where.

Alarm pulses a little bit stronger. Maybe I shouldn't have been so quick to boot Wilbur off my case.

And I *definitely* should have taken the car.

Swallowing, I consider asking somebody for help and then realise that I don't have the language skills to do that. I try to remember what Guides and Brownies taught me and realise I don't have a compass or dots helpfully indicating scattered trees or forested areas, and I can't use the stars for navigation.

Which means Nat was right: they are *not* transferable skills at all.

Then – with a sigh of frustration and an inward curse at the Brown Owl who invented the useless 'Out and About' badge – I give up and head towards the barriers with my useless map flapping.

It'll start making sense at some point, I'm absolutely sure of it.

Sooner or later it has to, right?

Everything will land sunny side up: all I need to do is stay positive.

Here's what I learnt in Year 7 physics:

In any atom, there is a nucleus containing protons and

neutrons, and a number of electrons spiralling around the outside. If the atom gains electrons, the atom becomes negatively charged, and if it loses electrons it becomes positively charged.

Therefore positive attracts negative, and vice versa.

Which explains why the next hour unravels so quickly.

I'm drawing all the bad luck in the entire Northern Hemisphere to me with my hopeful, sunny vibes.

Sweating, I run like a rabid mouse around the Métro.

Round and round; hopping on trains and off again, going up and down escalators, peering at maps and the fronts of trains and the faces of other commuters, panic rising by the minute and probably – although I don't have time to check – frothing slightly at the mouth.

Stopping to have a nibble of a chocolate bar on the way because it's important to keep my blood sugar levels stable when my adrenaline is spiking uncontrollably.

And also because French chocolate is *really* nice.

But it's no good.

I am thoroughly and comprehensively lost.

"*Excusez-moi,*" I finally say after two hours and ten minutes, pulling urgently on the arm of a ticket inspector, now back at my original station, "*Où est la Porte d'Auteuil?*"

I've asked six people so far, and my French accent is apparently so horrible I got sent to *Porte De Montreuil,* which is on totally the other side of Paris.

I can't believe I spent five years studying *German.*

"*Eh?*" he says, staring at the map I'm desperately flapping in his face. "*La Porte d'Auteuil?*"

"Mmmm," I blurt, face red and flustered. "*S'il vous plaît, pardon.* Quickly, *s'il vous plaît. Pardon.*"

I'm so agitated now that the only words I can remember in French are *please* and *sorry:* the two cornerstones of my everyday vocabulary.

I glance at my watch.

It's six-thirty, and I was told to be at my second fashion show at six o' clock, *on the dot.* I'm not sure how big a dot is, but I'm pretty sure it's not thirty minutes.

"*Marchez,*" he says, lifting his eyebrows.

I stare at him with round eyes. *March?*

"It's January," I say in slight frustration. "And I don't want to be rude, but I really don't think a conversation about the seasons right now is very helpful."

"*Marchez*," he says again, pointing to the ceiling and making little walking leg motions with his fingers. "*Vous pouvez y aller à pied.*"

À pied. Foot? Feet.

Oh my God, you have got to be kidding me: I can walk there on *foot*?

"How long will it take?" I say, grabbing my map, turning it round and looking at it again. I think maybe I've been holding it upside down this whole time. "Umm, *combien*?"

"*Neuf minutes*," he says in quite clear amusement. "*Mais cinq minutes…*" He wiggles his little walking-man fingers very quickly.

Five minutes.

I can be there in five minutes.

And I start running.

30

OK, just for fun I'm going to ask my question again.

What's the chance of me screwing up three times in twenty-four hours?

Answer: a hundred per cent.

According to statistics, there's a 96 per cent chance of surviving a plane crash, a 99 per cent chance of recovering from a bite by a poisonous spider and a 99.9999999999 per cent chance of getting through a train crash if you're sitting at the back.

Whereas the chance of Harriet Manners not making a big mistake while on a modelling trip at any given opportunity appears to be zero.

And I'd really like to stay sunny and positive at all times:

bright in the face of trials, hopeful when confronted with tribulations.

But that is *not* reassuring maths.

Breathing hard, six minutes later I run up the road towards a bright yellow and black building as swarms of people begin to enter the front doors and take their seats.

"*Excuse me*," a lady in a gigantic electric-blue fur coat says crossly as I burst past her, muttering *sorry sorry sorry* for the millionth time today. "Do you know what a queue is?"

"Of course," I say politely over my shoulder, panting. "It's a line or sequence of people, and etymologically it derives from the old French word *cue* or *coe*, which means *tail*."

I mean, we're in France.

You'd think she'd already know that.

Then I push through the crowd a little harder, still saying *sorry sorry sorry* as quickly as I can.

"Harriet Manners," I blurt urgently to the man standing in the reception as my face heats up to boiling point. "I'm one of the models and I'm late. There was a…" I pause, wondering how to explain that I've spent the entire day so far underground, like a mole. "I'm just late," I finish weakly. "Sorry."

"You should have come through the back door with the others," he says with a disapproving frown. "But OK. Quickly."

Nodding at his colleague, he leads me through.

My phone is buzzing, so I quickly grab it and stare at the screen:

Blueberrypop! Versace LOVES ME! Look! There safely? All spangletastic? F-G xxx

Attached is a photo of Wilbur, beaming and holding up a purple and orange handbag with a Medusa clasp.

I smile, then swallow.

I'm here. Whether or not I'm safe and/or spangletastic remains to be seen.

Arrived in one piece! :) Hxx

It's handy to be uber-literal sometimes.

"You!" a woman shouts as I'm ushered with flappy hands into a chaotic back room. "Are you Harriet Manners?"

According to www.howmanyofme.com, there are 90,262 Harriets in America, 2,360 people with the surname Manners and only one with both.

I really wish that was me right now.

"Y-yes," I stammer. "I'm really sorry, I had a map but there wasn't a compass and I—"

"Don't care," she says, grabbing me by the arm. "Save the excuses for your agent. We need you ready *now*."

Beetroot, damp and throbbing in the face, I'm dragged through an assorted variety of models backstage so beautiful it feels a bit like being thrown into the most stunning and elegant chocolate box in the world.

They're all totally perfect.

There is every shade of skin colour possible, hair colour and texture, eye colour, nose shape: all different expressions of natural beauty, and each equally spectacular.

Every shade apart from fluorescent red, anyway.

Apparently that's just me.

But if my previous show was a dark, Henry James short story from the land of Gothic nightmares, this is the light opposite.

Just like chocolates, every model is wearing a different vivid colour: bright, flamboyant shades in ruffles and frills and shiny satins. There are explosions of greens and peaches and baby blues and yellows everywhere, and if I look closely, every dress is covered in tiny tropical prints.

One girl in an elaborately long green number is covered in miniature toucans, another in orange has pink flamingos, while a girl having her shoes put on for her is covered in teeny tiny limes.

For a show set in January, it's decidedly exotic.

It's dark and cold outside, but I can almost *feel* the sunshine.

"In," the stylist says, holding out a turquoise and floaty calf-length dress: it sticks out from the waist in a bell shape and is covered in teeny little yellow pineapples.

Obediently and quietly, I undress and get in.

I'm zipped up and straightened out.

Then I glance around. The other models are starting to line up towards a door and I haven't even looked in a mirror yet. At least now my face is a throbbing dark pink I'm contributing to the glorious rainbow spectrum.

And I've totally missed the show briefing.

I guess *the dot* was smaller than I'd hoped.

"But my hair?" I blurt as plastic blue wellies are unceremoniously shoved on my feet like a naughty toddler at playtime and I'm pushed towards the other models. "My make-up? Don't I need... temporarily enhancing? Umm, de-brightening slightly?"

"No," the woman says sharply. "Thank God." Then she turns her attention to a model behind me fiddling with one of her dress straps.

"GIRL!" somebody screams in a voice I recognise instantly. "People just *can't keep us apart,* right? We're like, what's the word I'm looking for?"

"Peas in a pod?" the model behind us suggests helpfully.

"Oh my God," Kenderall sighs loudly. "What an imagination. No, really. Your brain is *sooooo* unique." She rolls her eyes then charges towards me in a peach gown, ignoring the complaints of a diminutive woman with a little earpiece. "We're like *beans in a tin, babe.*"

Then she grabs me in a one-armed, kiwi-print hug.

"Kenderall," a woman says in exasperation.

"It's *Siren* now."

"*Siren.* Get back in your position, please, and stop crushing your outfit. We're about to go on."

"*Sheesh,*" Kenderall sighs. "I know what I'm doing, lady. Siren is not an amateur. I look *much* better when contrasted with somebody shorter and less toned, like Harriet here. Let the professionals *work.*"

The woman opens her mouth, then shuts it again and decides to invest her energy somewhere more productive. With a resigned grimace, she goes back to arranging the less noisy girls instead.

Still trying to adjust to the backstage whirlwind – and also yet another dig at my lack of stature – I blink at Kenderall.

Then at what she's holding under her spare arm.

Again at what she's holding.

Then again.

I think the accelerated blood flow caused by running must have affected my eyesight, because she appears to be holding an enormous, papier-mâché-and-foam stag head. The antlers are four feet across, it's covered all over in pale pink velvet and there are small round holes covered in thin, black netting where the eyes would be.

For want of a better way of describing it, it's like looking at a grown-up Bambi.

After the scene that makes everyone cry.

"What–" I say, licking my lips. "Uh, Ken— Siren, why have you…"

Then I look at the floor. Lining the wall, neatly, is a row of giant animal heads.

Badgers, skunks, foxes, owls, squirrels.

All in pastel velvets – lavenders, creams, blues – with blank, unseeing netted eyes and furry little noses.

"Weird, huh," Kenderall says, lifting the stag head and putting it over her own. "I mean," she continues, slightly muffled. "Why you'd want to cover up the perfect and peerless face God gave me I have no idea. Good thing I've got the hot body too."

205

One by one, the other models are putting their velvet/papier-mâché heads on as well. Like *The Animals of Farthing Wood* crossed with a My Little Pony nightmare.

I stare at the disembodied head next to me.

It's a pale yellow rabbit, with a little pink nose and enormous, three-foot floppy yellow velvet ears sticking out of the top.

Now I *really really* wish I had been at the briefing.

On the upside, I do like rabbits.

They have 360-degree panoramic vision, can hear in two directions at once and are capable of jumping a very long way to safety, very quickly.

Maybe I'll be able to now too.

"OK, girls!" the lady cries jauntily. "Remember what we told you! Good luck! And remember – *stay dry*!"

There's a laugh, and bouncy music I recognise from Nat's bedroom kicks in, with an additional electronic beat that pounds through the building.

What is happening?

WHAT DID THEY TELL US?

The door opens and with a wave of alarm I see the

bright, sparkling turquoise light of an enormous, empty swimming pool.

"Show time!"

31

It's a well-documented fact that I'm a creature of planning.

I like my lists, my itineraries, my schedules, my mapped-out pictures of exactly where my friends will sit when we eat pizza. In fact, I get quite cross when they try to change the order without asking first.

Attention to detail is one of my most endearing qualities.

But even though I obviously knew I was coming to the *Piscine Molitor* – built in the 1920s and famous for both the unveiling of the world's first modern bikini and giving its name to the protagonist in *Life of Pi* – I assumed we would be modelling *around* it.

As none of us are capable of walking on the surface of water like either Jesus or Pygmy Geckos.

Except that – as the door continues to swing open and shut and the girls begin to walk out, one by one – it's becoming rapidly clear that the catwalk runs *through the swimming pool.*

Or, more specifically, two inches *below* it.

Just under the surface of the enormous, rectangular, fluorescent blue water is a long white stage, surrounded by lights that illuminate the entire building and flick shimmering rainbows on to the white, art-deco walls and ceilings.

Around the edges are palm trees, scattered at random and hung with tiny brightly coloured party lights. They blink all the way across the balconies, where hundreds of fashion people are sitting in sunglasses, furs, scarves, heels, chatting and laughing: quietly buzzing with excitement.

Along the edges of the pool, photographers are eagerly clustered.

And models are just *splashing through.*

Confidently striding to the music: kicking down the middle, stomping the flashing, drenched catwalk as water and lights spray everywhere.

Wearing tropical, floaty dresses.

And giant forest animal heads.

And *plastic wellies.*

Because apparently this is what happens at Paris Couture Week.

Swallowing, I focus a bit harder and try to remember how to breathe. And how to swallow, because frankly I'm having difficulty.

The models appear to be prancing to the bottom of the catwalk, pausing with a hand on their hip, turning left and turning right, pausing again and then kicking straight back, by then soaked to the skin.

That seems pretty simple.

It's the *only* thing about this situation that does.

"Game on," Stag-Kenderall says, holding her hand up to high-five me. "And remember to keep your head, babe. Lolz."

I grab my yellow giant bunny and stick it on anxiously.

Yup.

Keeping my head.

Easier said than done.

32

Scientists have studied how we walk.

Apparently by analysing more than 100,000 pressure points created by our feet, they are able to pinpoint seventy key patterns unique to an individual.

It's so accurate that they can correctly identify people from their stroll 99.6 per cent of the time.

Without even seeing their faces.

All I'm going to say is: I really hope none of them are in the audience right now. Kenderall may not like having her *visage* hidden, but I'm kind of a big fan.

At terrifying times like this, being anonymous could have its advantages.

The door opens.

Holding my breath, I walk with intention on to the

catwalk: shoulders back, chin up. The foam-and-papier-mâché rabbit head is surprisingly heavy, but as long as I keep my neck very still and stay facing the end of the catwalk, I can focus on the gravity situated round my bellybutton and keep my ears balanced vertically.

Which is definitely not something I've said before.

As fiercely as I can, I begin to stomp through the water in my wellies.

Trying to copy the red squirrel who went before me, I kick my feet as if I'm back at home: walking to school through autumn leaves, trying to find the best and biggest conkers to fight with.

The music pounds, water sprays.

Lights are flashing, but through the tiny netted eyeholes of the rabbit head I can't really tell from where. I'm moving too fast: it's just a mass of blinding, sparkling flares from across the audience seated in a nearly 360-degree circle. All hanging over the balconies, built specifically to look like those of an old cruise liner, back in the swinging twenties.

Around my feet is a bright turquoise swimming pool.

Somewhere up ahead is an open sky.

But I can't risk looking either upwards or downwards.

Instead, I focus through the two little round holes, into the net-spangled space in front of me. I slam my feet down, feeling the cold water spraying and my huge velvet ears flopping with every step.

Finally, I reach the end of the catwalk.

I manage to stop before I plunge off the end, put my hand on my hip and pause just long enough for another flurry of sparkles to disorientate me.

I face the other way for a few seconds.

Then I start stomping back through the water like Gene Kelly in *Singin' In The Rain,* or maybe a baby elephant on its first outing at a watering hole.

A sudden thrill of pride, triumph and amazement surges through me.

I did it!

I totally nailed that fashion job!

On the dot, I reckon.

Mentally, I high-five myself.

I do a little inward Happy Dance, so tiny nobody can see it.

Then, dripping and victorious, I make my way through the door and wait in a shivering line of forest animals. Let's just say that January, floaty summer dresses and chlorinated water are not a comfortable combination.

I can feel myself starting to grin.

"You know," Kenderall says loudly as she stands next to me, water droplets collecting at the end of her antlers, "I fail to see the *point* in paying models of *our* stature, fame and *versatility* to do a show where you can't see who we are."

"*Siren*," the stylist behind her admonishes.

"*What*, babe?" Kenderall says fearlessly. "I mean, you could get any old skinny girl to do this. My face is *extraordinary.* You are *wasting* these cheekbones."

My happy smile gets wider: there's actually something kind of refreshing about a beautiful girl who knows she's beautiful.

A few minutes later, the door opens again.

And in a long line, we all go out together: splashing back out through the swimming pool and stopping less than a metre from each other.

Relaxing now, I watch what everyone else is doing.

They're not posing: they're just standing very still, with their feet at shoulders' distance apart, their arms by their sides like mannequins.

So I do the same.

Beaming happily from ear to ear, I face the front with my back straight.

With a *bang*, small pieces of coloured confetti begin to explode around us: perfectly in time to the music, flying into the sky with majestic rainbow *pops*.

Now I'm not stomping and there isn't water splashing up everywhere, I can see a lot more clearly through my eyeholes. Through the colourful tissue-paper clouds, into the audience, up into the rafters, to the people lined up along the front.

There's an almost static-like buzz in the air: crackling and making every one of my five million hair follicles stand on end yet again. Everyone is chatting, leaning forward, taking photos, laughing. Enjoying themselves in one big, glorious fashion party.

No one can see my massive smile as I let my eyes slide over the congregation.

Another thrill of warmth rushes through me.

You know what?

I don't get invited to parties very often but it's a shame, because I think I'd really enjoy them. I feel vibrant. Included. Part of something bigger than just myself.

I didn't realise Fashion Week could be like this. So bright and fun, such a celebration of creativity.

No *wonder* Nat was excited for me.

My eyes make one more glorious and victorious sweep of the pool, drinking everything in.

Then they stop.

And the whole universe stops with them.

We each blink on average eight hundred million times in a lifetime, but – as my entire body and every muscle in it slowly freezes – there's a chance I may never shut my eyes again.

33

___

In the middle of all the chaos and noise – in the very centre of the colour and light and pop and explosions – is a boy.

He's sitting very still.

His skin is brown, his hair is curly.

His lips are wide and curve upwards in the corners: there's a mole on his left cheek, and holes in his jeans. His eyes are black and tilted, and they blink slightly too slowly.

He's too far away, but I know that if I got closer he'd smell green: like limes, and grass and summer leaves. I know his hands are warm and dry, and that his fingers somehow fit mine perfectly.

That he moves lazily, with power and purpose.

Like a big, dark lion.

I know exactly what his face looks like when he's sleepy, when he's sad, when he's happy, when he's proud: what

he looks like when he's been laughing for so long that little lines have creased into the corners of his eyes.

Except I've never seen this expression before.

Never seen his face so motionless.

The average fully grown human head weighs about five kilograms. Our brains weigh about 1.3 kilograms, and then the rest of it is composed of skull, of teeth, of facial muscles and blood and skin. Some of which I've seen pretty close-up today already.

But as I stare unblinking at the boy in the crowd, it feels like mine is about to crumple: folding inward on itself like a piece of origami paper, the way it did when I first met him.

I'm going to literally lose my head.

And – judging by the way he's leaning forward, dark eyes staring somehow at, through and into my huge rabbit mask – the feeling is mutual.

He's here. This time it's really him. I can see Nick.

And Nick can see me.

34

Time is not constant.

According to Einstein's theory of relativity, the closer something is to the centre of the earth, the slower time goes: the day stretches fractionally longer for our feet than it does for our brains.

As I stand on the stage and stare directly at Nick – as he sits and stares directly at me – I think I must be miles and miles underground for the third time today.

Everything, now, has stopped.

It's not just me and him any more. It's as if every atom in the room has paused with us: bright confetti, hovering in mid-air; people frozen with their mouths open; water stiffened and solid, camera bulbs in one blanket of light.

Nick's here.

He's here he's here he's here…

And I can feel a loud banging starting inside my head, travelling with thuds through my body, like Edgar Allan Poe's famous *Tell-tale Heart.*

Our eyes are locked: I can't move my head, I can't breathe, my ears have gone numb.

He's here he's here he's here...

"Babe?"

Nick's just staring back.

He's here he's here he's here...

"Babe?"

Nick's here Nick's here Nick's here...

"Babe."

A hand grabs my arm, and without thinking I blink and twist in bewilderment towards it. With a soft, fluffy whallop, one of my big velvet bunny ears whacks the red squirrel next to me straight in the face.

"*Oi,*" a badger mutters under her breath as she starts to follow the rest of the forest, now clapping their hands and leaving the stage. "Watch it, Bunny."

I whip back towards her in confusion and feel a sharp tug on my head.

Still disorientated, I tug again.

Every vein in my body still empty, I turn blankly to where I'm stuck. Somehow – and I will never understand how this happened – one of my velvet rabbit ears has got caught on Kenderall's antlers.

"Get *off*," Kenderall hisses, pulling her head back sharply. "*Dude.*"

As she's pointed out more than once now, Kenderall is considerably bigger and stronger than me: before I know it I'm being effortlessly dragged three or four steps towards her, velvet bunny ear still attached to her head.

"I'm *trying*," I say, tugging back as hard as I can.

Kenderall tugs me again. "Try *harder*."

Lights are starting to flicker around us, and through the netted holes in my bunny headpiece I can see the other models are lurking at the back of the stage, unsure of whether to leave us mid-catwalk or not.

Somewhere in the midst of shock, my old friends Panic, Desperation and Humiliation are starting to rise like waves.

"Wait," I whisper, pulling again. "Kenderall, if you just stop I can try and disentangle…"

But it's too late.

With one more jerk of her head, the incredibly powerful Kenderall tugs backwards at exactly the same moment as I do.

For a fraction of a second, we both freeze in mid-air.

Exactly as the whole world did a moment ago.

Then there's a loud ripping sound, a squeak and a roar of rage.

Followed by an almighty splash.

35

—

Or more specifically, *two* almighty splashes.

I go straight into the deep end of the swimming pool first, followed closely by a loudly bellowing Kenderall.

And the chances that I'll screw up *four* times in twenty-four hours?

All of them.

For a moment, I'm so humiliated and ashamed I strongly consider just swimming to the bottom of the pool and sitting down there for as long as I can.

Unfortunately, my costume makes that impossible.

Under the cosy velvet my papier-mâché-and-foam rabbit head is forming an ad-hoc buoyancy aid: dragging me to the surface and leaving me stuck there for all eternity.

Bobbing away, for everyone to stare at.

Through the little netted eyeholes, I can see that Kenderall is treading water with her antlers wobbling like a Disney out-take edit.

I guess it figures that I'm Thumper.

There's a tense pause.

Then the crowd suddenly erupts in excitement and applause: lights flashing, people shouting, the music mixing with cheers and yells.

"*BABE*," Kenderall shouts to me in the middle of the chaos as I wince and mentally prepare myself to have my head ripped off both verbally and physically, "you are a branding *genius*. You should have let me know this was your plan. I'd have been *so* behind it. Nobody will *ever forget us again.*"

Then, with a grin, she triumphantly yanks off her deer head and waves at the crowd like a dripping-wet homecoming queen.

"*Go*," someone is shouting desperately from behind us on the stage. "Just *get in too.*"

With a loud splash, the badger jumps in.

Then the owl, followed by a fox.

A squirrel and bear.

Moose, wolf, mouse, hedgehog.

Splash, splash, splash, splash.

Until the majority of a deciduous forest is swimming in the water next to us. Somebody has obviously decided that it's better to embrace the chaos than try to stop it: to make this look like the finale spectacle they had actually planned.

And I know I should feel guilty.

I should feel responsible for screwing up their original programme, or for forcing thirty-five models to go for an impromptu and freezing-cold winter swim.

But I don't.

As the lights flash and the crowd shouts – as the rainbow confetti continues to shower down on our heads like bright rain – I can feel the warm grin start to spread across my face again.

Wider and wider, until it feels like it's going to split me in two: as if maybe it already has.

Nick came back.

He was there, against all odds: he saw me and he knew me, the way he always has.

For those few seconds we were us again.

So it doesn't matter that he's gone now; it doesn't matter that I can't see him in the crowd any more, and I don't know when I next will.

As I lie on my back in the water and stare at the stars, glowing steadily in the darkness, I'm suddenly surer than I've ever been that this isn't the end.

It never really was.

Because the very last thing I saw before I fell in the water was Lion Boy looking straight at me.

And smiling.

Read on to see Harriet through Nick's eyes – the very first time they met...

NICK

—

I really don't want to be here.

In fact, I've spent the last six hours thinking about it carefully, and there are roughly a hundred other things I'd rather be doing on a cold Thursday morning in the middle of December.

Getting chased by a seagull the size of a tiger.

Slipping and smashing my head on a rock and waking up to find the seagull sitting directly on my chest, staring at me with one black, beady eye.

Looking round and seeing it's part of a seagull gang.

And *none* of those hundred things involve sitting in an enormous exhibition centre in Birmingham, packed with clothes and lipsticks and necklaces.

At least the huge space can just about contain Wilbur.

"…and I said to her *KABOOM!*" he shouts loudly,

exploding from his seat and throwing his hands into the air like a Jack-In-A-Box without a box. "Those shoes are *turquoise not green,* and I defy you to argue with my epic colour-wheel key-ring, Stephanie! I am a teapot of majesty and you are not! Put that in your log-burning stove and smoke it!"

I slump a bit further in my chair.

Today is sucking even harder than I thought it would, and the Suckiness Expectations were pretty high in the first place.

When I agreed to this, Wilbur *promised* me it would take half an hour, max. "Just pop in for thirty minutes, Nick," were his precise words. "It will be the work of a moment, my unfairly handsome koala-bean."

All I'm going to say is: I've known Wilbur Evans since I was eight years old, when he used to let me play my Game Boy under his agency desk while my aunt Yuka 'babysat' me (ignored me completely and bribed me not to tell my mum). And this is my fourth full day here, with no apparent end in sight.

Thirty-three dull-as-hell hours, feeling like the world's biggest idiot.

Frankly, I should have known better.

Still way too overexcited, Wilbur spins in a circle with his bright yellow jacket flaring out. "Ooh!" he says on his third rotation, slamming to a stop and grabbing my arm abruptly. "Peanut-button, I see a Potential!"

I reluctantly pivot my eyes slowly to the side without even bothering to move my head.

There's a beautiful girl a few metres away: standing with one leg bent slightly in front of the other, one hand on her hip and her chin tipped upwards. She's pouting and pretending to carefully assess a stall full of accessories without physically moving her eyeballs.

Every now and then – when she thinks we can't see her – she flicks a glance in the direction of the Infinity stall.

She knows that nobody *actually* stands like that, right?

I mean, I've been a part of the fashion industry in one way or another my entire life and I can tell you with some confidence that nobody stands with a hip randomly jutted out and a face like a fish when they're watching television.

"Nope," I say tiredly, folding my arms.

"No?" Wilbur says anxiously, peering a bit closer. "Are

you sure? Nicholas, my six-packed bunny of glory, do I need to remind you exactly what's hanging on this? One more selection mistake and I'm out. My last choice of new girl turned out to be thirty-seven years old and it did *not* go down well."

"I know," I say, smiling a little. The agency went *ape.* "Trust me, Wil. That girl is not what Yuka's looking for. For another modelling job, definitely, but I know my aunt and that one is far too…"

We both peer at her as subtly as possible.

Bright blue eyes: piercing, even from ten metres away. Smooth, glossy golden tendrils; flawless, porcelain skin. Legs so long she looks slightly out of proportion, like a very pretty ostrich.

"Beautiful?" Wilbur suggests. "Naturally graceful? Aesthetically blessed with symmetry, bone structure and culturally revered facial features?"

"Aware of all of the above."

Wilbur laughs. "Go get her anyway, will you? Or I just *know* that Stephanie will get in there first, like a rabid terrier with a back-combed fringe."

And that's why I'm *really* here.

Wil's pretending to ask for my advice, but there's a bet on between him and his arch-nemesis – a particularly vicious strain of agent called Stephanie – to see who can find the new female face of Baylee first.

And he thinks I'm the Deciding Factor.

Partly because its creative director is my Aunty Yuka – famous for making ice queens look warm and cuddly – partly because she's already roped me into being the male face (for free, I should add) and partly because…

Well. Ahem.

"Darling," Wilbur explained when I finally realised what was going on: with horror, embarrassingly late. "Genetics gave you an unfair advantage on the rest of the human race that you neither deserved, earned, nor asked for. It's only fair that you pay a bit of that luck forward. To me, ideally."

"By *smarming* girls into signing with you first?"

"By leading them *to me* and *away* from Stephanie like a gorgeous, cheek-boned Pied Piper."

I stared at him in consternation.

"Wilbur, you do realise in that fairytale the Pied Piper led the children into a cave and they were *never seen again*?"

"Crikey," Wilbur said, looking bemused. "I don't remember that ending. Well don't *kill* them, Nick. Just give one of those fifteen-thousand-dollar grins, point them this way and let hormones and hope do the rest."

So that's what I've done.

For four days, I've been reluctantly and furiously thrown into a crowd of girls, repeatedly. And I've hated every single, cringing, morally dubious second of it.

I'm just pretending not to, for Wilbur's sake.

And also because it's kind of rude to show nice and totally faultless girls you'd rather be anywhere else on the planet but talking to them.

"Hey there," I say every time I'm pointed towards another Potential, plastering on a broad, fake smile. "I'm Nick Hidaka, and I'm with Infinity Models. Would you like to come with me?"

Like some kind of slimy Australian creep.

And what's worse: it *works*.

These sweet girls squeak in excitement, leave their friends behind and follow me without questions, without concern, without any deliberation or consideration or measures to check whether I'm actually telling the truth or not.

I don't even need a magic flute.

"Please?" Wilbur says again as I continue to scowl at him, still slumped. He widens his eyes like an owl. "Pretty please, Nikolai? With a blueberry on top? Just one more time?"

I freaking hate my job.

Unfortunately, Wilbur's helped me more than once over the last nine years and I kind of owe him this. Even when he makes my name Russian for no reason whatsoever.

"And then I can go home?"

"And then you can go home," he confirms cheerfully. "Or to that model flat in London that Infinity is totally overcharging you for."

"Fine," I sigh, standing up and rubbing my neck. "But if this is the wrong girl *again* and Yuka blames me for it *again* and stops all my Christmas gifts for the next six years, you *will* replace them."

"Done," Wilbur agrees in delight, shoving me gently with his hand. "And stop grumping, Nickerbocker. Dark and broody is *so* passé."

I laugh. "I'm not grumping, *William*. I'm responding to a horrible and awkward situation in an appropriately unimpressed manner."

"Remember to tell her how pretty she is. They like to hear that. I'd do it myself but I'm in my twenties so I can't without sounding scary."

I look drily at Wilbur – he's forty-six, for the record – and then at the gorgeous blonde, now surreptitiously gazing at her own reflection in her handbag clasp. "Something tells me she already knows."

With a grimace, I slap my widest, most charming grin on.

And I try my very hardest to look like I mean it.

*

I know what you might think of me already, by the way: that I'm an arrogant, superficial idiot.

And, honestly – if you do – I really don't blame you.

It kind of comes with the modelling territory.

Just so you know, I didn't always look like this.

At primary school in Northern Australia, I was the kid who got hassled daily for being really small: for having a big mouth that didn't fit his face and *slanty* eyes and *yellow* skin and a black frizz-ball for a head, and for having a mum who didn't speak any English at parent–teacher evenings and instead chattered away in "Oriental" (it was Japanese, but five-year-olds don't always care about silly little details like my racial and cultural background).

Then I hit thirteen and – like basically every other teenage boy who lives in a sun-kissed coastal town – I discovered a love of surfing.

I stretched out a bit (thanks, testosterone, and Dad's genes).

And the next thing I knew, I was six-foot-three, my hair had finally chilled out, my mouth fit my face better and the designer aunt who had left me under desks all my life suddenly wanted me out in the spotlight to "do a few photos for her, here and there".

Which led to a few more: a lot more *there* than *here*.

The next thing I knew, I was being dragged out of my life in Australia like I was on a riptide: swept away on a huge wave I didn't see coming or want or know what to do with. And couldn't seem to get off again.

Which for a surfer, is pretty ironic.

Cue: public recognition, money in the bank, and the general assumption that I must be an idiot, because I'm 'that guy' so why wouldn't I be?

I'm a successful model because of who I'm related to.

Because of what I happen to look like.

Because I must be too thick to do anything more important or substantial, and honestly they may have a point on that one: I missed most of my exams in a three-year whirlwind of fashion shoots and shows, and I can't take that back.

Which is exactly why I've decided the Baylee campaign is going to be my very last modelling job.

Ever.

I have no idea what I'm going to do next – apart from going home and getting straight back into the sea – but all I'm sure of is that there has to be more to being seventeen than *this.*

Now it's just a few more steps to final freedom.

"OhmyGodohmyGod," a girl squeaks loudly as I try to make a wide circle around a small group, like some kind of wary and dubious shark. "He's *coming this way...*"

From behind me I feel a sharp tug at my T-shirt sleeve, and the sound of a slight rip. "I just *touched* him..."

Another prod. "I'm *never washing my hand again.*"

"Quickly, get a selfie of me with him in the background!"

Bring on the seagulls.

"Hey there," I say, tapping the blonde girl on the shoulder and trying to feel a bit less like an automated Ken doll. "My name is—"

She spins round with a startlingly pretty, dimpled smile. "Nick Hidaka," she says smoothly. "Oh, I know who you are and why you're here."

"Right," I say, frowning a little despite myself.

"Gucci, summer season," she continues, flicking her gold hair out of her eyes with a little head-toss. "Prada, winter campaign. You're with Infinity, aren't you. You want me to model, don't you."

There are no question marks at all. Her confidence is impressive, but also kind of alarming.

At least she's done the hard work for me.

"Yep," I say in relief, because that means – *thank you thank you thank you* – I'm finally done for the day. "Or at least talk to you about Infinity. Our stall's over there. If you just want to come with—"

Then I abruptly stop.

My eyes have accidentally drifted over her shoulder and, without warning, suddenly stuck: held firmly, like magnets.

"With you?" she finishes, gently touching my arm. "Of *course*. I'm Poppy, by the way. I'm actually already modelling – that probably goes without saying – but I'd be *very* interested in switching agencies. I just don't think I'm getting the high-grade campaigns I should be aiming for, you know?"

"I..." With an effort, I drag my eyes back to her. Did she just ask me a question? "You're... I'm sorry, what did you say?"

"I'm Poppy."

"Who?"

"*Poppy.* Like the flower?"

I blink and my eyes drift back over her shoulder again.

She's standing maybe fifteen metres away: composed almost entirely of coats. Her yellow puffa jacket is so large and round she looks a bit like a bumblebee, there's a second fluffy coat in her arms and chunky black cardigan piled on top, and she appears to be wearing a football kit.

Knee-length white socks and blue trainers, shiny neon-green shorts and a scratchy-looking orange nylon T-shirt with a large number seven drawn on it.

On top of her head is a large floppy blue hat covered in big pink flowers.

Honestly, she's dressed like the kind of crazy person you cross the road to avoid in case they randomly stab your leg with a pencil or corner you in an hour-long conversation about bus timetables.

But none of this is what I'm staring at.

It's her face that has stopped me mid-sentence.

Shadowed by the wide brim of the hat, it's small and sharply heart-shaped – pointed at the chin and curved round to a little widow's peak at the top – pale and rosy-cheeked and scattered with freckles. She has a slightly too-small nose, a sweet, gentle mouth, and bright, almost cartoon-like eyes: enormous and shining and vivid green.

She's undoubtedly pretty – in a strange, quiet way – but it's more than that. There's something… eloquent about her. Luminous and delicate, like a character from *A Midsummer's Night's Dream*.

And she's totally furious.

Her arms are crossed and she's glaring around the room with a deep, fierce scowl, as if she can't believe she's been dragged here either.

For the first time today, I've just seen something unexpected.

"*Hello?*" Poppy prods my arm, a tiny bit too hard. "Earth to Nick? Are we going to the model stall now? I can't *wait* to be introduced properly."

"Sure." I drag my eyes back to Poppy, as if they're on lead weights. Her dimples swiftly appear again, but not before I see a terrifyingly impatient muscle in her jaw jump. "Just give me a minute."

Frowning, I look past her again.

It's a good thing the girl in the football kit has turned away and started examining hats on the stall behind her, because I'm beginning to feel like a total stalker.

Stop staring, Nick.

You're being massively uncool.

Pouting her lip-glossed lips, Poppy follows my gaze then gives a sharp little laugh.

"Eww, who brought the bag-lady? Doesn't she know this is a *fashion* event? What was she even *thinking* when she got dressed this morning?"

"Maybe about something other than herself," I say flatly, breaking away. "The Infinity stall's just behind you, Poppy. I'm sure you'll do brilliantly. Good luck."

And before I can process what's happening – or why I've just totally overreacted – I'm walking towards the girl by the hat stall with no idea of what I'm going to do.

Or what I'm going to say.

*

Which is not a problem.

Mainly because this girl has apparently taken all the possible words available in the English language already.

As I get closer, I hear her voice.

It's silvery, bell-like, clear and old-fashioned. Every word is formed carefully and neatly, with precision. As if she's from a different time: parachuted in from the nineteenth century by accident.

And it literally doesn't stop.

It lilts up and down and round and round and just keeps going, like light, bouncy music. Despite the totally blank expression of the shoppers next to her and the sighs of the people trying to get to a popular make-up stand on the other side.

With unabashed enthusiasm, she picks a red beret off the stall and chirpily informs everybody in the immediate vicinity that the earliest record of hat-wearing comes from a cave in Lussac-les-Chateaux, fifteen thousand years ago, and that Vikings never *actually* wore horned helmets and isn't that interesting?

All signs of her fury, fifteen seconds ago, are gone: her anger already forgotten.

I feel my nose twitch.

This is clearly not a girl who holds on to a mood.

"Excuse me," I hear the unimpressed woman behind the hat stall demand as I approach quietly from the side, "can you read?"

"Yes," the girl replies in surprise, nodding. "Very well, actually. My reading age is over twenty. But thank you for asking."

For the first time today, a genuine grin starts to stretch across my face. The woman's expression wavers – unsure whether she's being mocked or not – and then goes puce.

"Really? Can you read that sign there? Read it out loud."

"Of course," the girl agrees sweetly. "It says *Don't Touch The Hats...*" She glances at the beret, still clutched in her hand. "Oh."

"That's a hat," the woman snarls, pointing at it. "And *that*'s a hat. And you're touching them *all over.*"

OK, I think this is my chance.

This is the perfect opportunity to jump in, interrupt with *Hey there, I'm Nick Hidaka and I'm with Infinity Models,* save this girl from an unnecessary level of wrath and then somehow lead her away to Wilbur. She's definitely a Potential: she has an innocent, fairy-like daintiness that is *exactly* what Yuka has been searching for. She just needs to wear an outfit that isn't a football kit.

Except for some reason, I can't do it.

There's something stopping me. And it's not because she doesn't have the right look, it's…

I don't know what it is, but I just can't.

More importantly, I'm suddenly no longer sure if I *should*.

Instead, I feel myself take a step away.

"Sorry," the girl replies, abruptly grabbing the floppy hat off her head as her cheeks begin to go a pretty shade of pink. A fluffy mass of bright red hair shoots out from underneath, tied up with the kind of straggly green hair elastic that indicates she thinks that if she can't see the back of her head it doesn't exist. "It's, erm, very… *hatty.*"

At which point a pink flower promptly falls off.

Then another flower. And another. And a fourth: until all the flowers that were on the hat are lying in a pile at her feet.

There's a long silence.

The kind of silence that indicates that these kind of silences happen quite regularly.

"That's a very interesting design concept," the redhead says finally, clearing her throat and taking a quick step backwards, nearly stepping on my feet. I scoot backwards again. "Self-detaching flowers? It's very modern."

"*They're not self-detaching*," the woman hisses. "*You detached them.* And now you're going to have to pay for it."

The girl takes another step backwards.

Ditto, me.

"You know," she says in her silvery voice, cheeks now starting to flame, "you're very lucky that hat didn't kill me. I could have choked on one of those flowers and died.

The playwright Tennessee Williams died from choking on a bottle cap. *Then* how would you have felt?"

"I'll take a cheque or credit card details."

"Tell you what, how about I forget that you tried to kill me if you forget that I broke your hat? How does that sound?"

"Pay for the hat."

"No."

"Pay for the hat."

"I *can't*."

"Pay for the h—"

And as the redhead takes one more, panicked step to the side, I see it happening just a fraction of a second too late. Before I can reach out a hand to grab her, she smashes – hard – into the corner of the L-shaped table.

For the briefest moment, she wobbles, paused in mid-air, eyes wide and mouth in an O shape.

Like an anime cat.

Then – with a loud *crash* – everything falls down.

*

And by 'everything' I mean *everything*.

The hat stall.

Every hat and fake plastic head on it. The stall next to it, and the stall next to that: three stalls in the opposite direction. A jug of water, perched precariously on a chair, and a clothing rod which has just shattered a stall full of hand-painted mirrors and light bulbs.

There's ink and water and clothes and flowers and sequins and tables and barriers strewn everywhere, like the wreckage of some kind of fashion tsunami.

And in the middle is the redhead girl.

Sprawled in an awkward position: white football-socked legs in the air, face so dark with embarrassment her freckles look white, and her bright green eyes slowly filling with tears.

"I'm s-sorry," she mumbles over and over as the hat-stall owner screams at her. "I'm *so* sorry."

Then she glances in humiliation around her at the gathering crowd: eyes just missing mine by the tiniest fraction.

Something in my gut is starting to twist.

Every single instinct in me is telling me to reach forward

and pull her out, to block the voyeurs who are rubber-necking with no sensitivity or helping hands at all.

But it's too late.

If I grab her now, not only am I going to make her embarrassment worse – *hey! I'm a guy your age and I just saw you fall over and break everything ha ha ha!* – but I'm going to look like the worst kind of creep.

The dude who swoops in, an imaginary S drawn on his puffed-out chest: cape and ego flying and hands on his hips, inexplicably speaking in the third person.

Don't worry, young damsel in distress. Nick is here.

Nick shall save you.

I don't want to be that guy, but I also can't just leave her there.

I have to do *something*.

Abruptly, I turn and pound across the floor to Wilbur.

"Wil," I say, grabbing his arm without preamble, "come with me now."

Wilbur turns in obvious relief from a strained conversation of decreasing animation with Poppy, takes one look at the urgency written across my face and follows me.

"Her," I say, pointing into the middle of the hat stall chaos.

That's all I need to say.

*

I have no idea what to do next.

As Wilbur nods and launches abruptly towards her with his hand out – black hat bobbing – I turn away feeling surprisingly disorientated.

Where should I go?

I scan the crowd and make a snap decision: start striding through the crowds, automatically heading back to the Infinity stall, as if I'm being pulled there on a string.

Wilbur's going to return with the girl any minute, and for some reason I suddenly feel an urgent need to be there too. She is *exactly* what Yuka is looking for, and is about to be offered the opportunity of a lifetime.

So why do I feel so guilty?

Over the last four days, I've been telling myself – over and over again – that at least I'm helping: that the girls we pick *want* to be here. That we're giving them a dream I may not want, but they probably will.

But – as I spot Poppy, still pouting by the stall, and promptly swing behind a column so she can't see me – I realise that's exactly why I didn't grab the green-eyed girl immediately in the first place.

Something's telling me this is wrong.

That we might be inadvertently about to sweep this silvery-voiced, bright-faced girl away on a wave she won't know what to do with, won't know how to manage: that she won't just get carried away, she might go straight under.

And I don't want to do that to her.

I don't want to give her the crazy, disjointed, unstable life I've had for the last three years: the life I've been so desperately trying to hand back.

I glance around the Infinity stall. There's a lame rope barrier holding the crowds away, but no privacy on the raised stand: Poppy's eyes are subtly sweeping the crowd – trying to work out where Wilbur has gone – and any second now she's going to spot me.

From round the corner, I hear a clear and yet very shaky voice.

"M-my jeans had sick on them."

"My jeans had sick on them!" Wilbur repeats jubilantly. He's talking even louder than he usually does (and that's pretty loud): he's either silly excited or trying to warn me that they're coming. "I love it! Such an imagination!"

Feeling unexpectedly alarmed, I glance around again.

I need to be here, but not here at the same time. I need to check she's OK, without her knowing it. To make sure she's being looked after, without her realising someone's trying to. Without her knowing that what could be a major fork in the road of her life is completely my fault.

To my left, Poppy begins to tap her fingernails on her sleeve impatiently and her eyes start drifting towards me.

"Darling-foot," I hear Wilbur say to my right, even louder, "I think you might be about to make my career, my little Pot of Tigers."

Shoot. There's literally no other choice.

I glance down at the large table I helped Wilbur set up

this morning: covered in a white tablecloth, dozens of Polaroid photos of girls and pink authorisation forms.

Then I roll my eyes.

On the upside, at least I don't want to be attacked by seagulls any more.

And I drop under the table.

*

I probably should have done this days ago.

It's kind of nice under here.

Quiet. Calm. Cool. Nobody trying to rip off tiny pieces of my T-shirt to take home as a keepsake.

"Now," I hear Wilbur say and the sound of some coats being dumped on the floor, "stand there and look gorgeous."

"But..."

There's the familiar *click* of a Polaroid camera.

"Now turn to the side?"

From the two inches of space under the edge of the tablecloth, I can just about see Wilbur's shiny orange loafers – dancing around with the jubilation of somebody who knows he's won a bet – and a pair of blue trainers and the ankles of the white knee-high socks, completely stationary.

Wilbur tuts and moves the girl around.

"*Wilbur…*"

"Baby-pudding, you know you look just like a treefrog? Darling, you could climb up a tree with no help at all and I wouldn't be shocked in the slightest."

Nice, one, Wil.

There's not scaring girls away and then there's comparing them to a slimy green amphibian.

Although frogs *are* kind of adorable, so they do have *something* in common.

"I have to go," the girl says, panic audibly rising. "I have to get out of here. I have to…"

And my former alarm pulses through me.

The blue trainers have suddenly moved closer to the table, and I stare at them in concern. Where's she headed? There's nothing in this direction but wall and table.

I watch as they move a little bit closer again.

Wait, she's not going to…

I mean, there's no way on earth she would…

Oh my God, is she actually going to…

Yup.

Before I can do anything, the girl drops to her knees and crawls under the table next to me.

*

Well, this is awkward.

For a few seconds, we blink at each other in surprise.

Up close, her face is even more incredible.

Her skin is so pale it's almost transparent, and it's scattered all over with pale gold flecks. Her large, intelligent eyes tilt down at the inner corners and are dozens of greens – moss and olive and teal – starred with pale, light gold eyelashes, giving her a faraway, distant expression.

Her top lip lifts up a fraction, her ears are very slightly pointed, and the mop of wavy, bright red hair is entirely escaping from the green hairband: curls shooting out around her face.

She smells of something pink and powdery, like sugar mice.

But it's the movement of her face that makes her more than pretty.

I can literally see emotions running across it like ripples: thoughts flickering through the water like fish.

It's totally fascinating.

And with a bolt of horror, I realise I've been examining her in silence for at least four seconds and if I don't say something quickly, she's going to think I'm some kind of troll hiding under a bridge and climb straight back out again.

"Hi," I say abruptly, reaching into my pocket, pulling out a piece of chewing gum and offering it to her like a cyborg vending machine.

She blinks at it and then at me.

OK, where did *that* come from? What is this sudden urge to give her a random gift? What am I, a giant cat?

With questioning eyes she assesses me carefully.

"Well?" I say as the awkwardness kicks up another notch. "Do you want the gum or not?"

Nice one, Nick. Make that offer worse by sounding vaguely aggressive and obsessed with chewy snacks.

How long has it been in there, anyway?

I'm pretty sure I haven't chewed gum for at least a month.

"I can see," I continue, nose starting to twitch, "that it's an extremely important decision and you need to think about it carefully. So I'll give you a few more seconds to weigh up the pros and cons."

"Chewing gum is banned in Singapore," she says out of the blue, frowning cutely. "Completely banned."

"Are we in Singapore?" I say, trying to make light of this curveball. "How long have I been asleep? How fast does this table move?"

I haven't been asleep, obviously, but how else do I explain being under here?

"No," she whispers, cheeks flaming. "We're still in Birmingham. I'm just making the point that if we *were* in Singapore, we could be arrested for even having chewing gum in our possession."

I can feel a grin pulling at my face again, so I make a huge effort to flatten it back out.

I love the way she seems to take everything so literally.

"Is that so?"

"Yes. Luckily we're not in Singapore, so you're safe."

"Well, thank God for UK legislation," I smile, then close my eyes so I can get my mouth under control again.

There's a short silence.

"I'm Harriet Manners," she says after a few seconds.

Harriet Manners.

"Hello, Harriet Manners."

"Have you been here long?"

"About half an hour," I lie.

"Why?"

Because I wanted to see you again. "I'm hiding from Wilbur. He's using me as bait. He keeps chucking me into the crowd to see how many pretty girls I can come back with."

"Like a maggot?"

I laugh. *Spot on.* "Yes. Pretty much exactly like a maggot."

"And have you… caught anything yet?"

"I'm not sure yet." I open one eye and look straight at her. Her eyes are warm, and my stomach feels exactly the way it does when I'm surfing: as if I've gone aerial, as if it's flying through the air, weightless. *I hope so.* "It's too early to say."

"Oh." She glances at a watch with a knife and fork on it instead of hands. "It's not that early. Actually, it's nearly lunchtime."

Quickly, I close my eyes before I laugh again.

That's literally the best watch I've ever seen.

"Do you often hide under furniture?" she asks curiously after another few seconds.

"I don't make a habit of it," I admit, grinning widely. "You?"

"All of the time. *All* of the time."

Then she sucks in her breath loudly.

I open my eyes a tiny crack: just wide enough to watch with curiosity as something flickers across her expression, diving in and out, struggling to the surface and dipping away again.

Then there's the sound of clipping and two red, glossy high-heeled shoes suddenly appear next to us, also paired with football socks.

"Harriet?" their owner says.

The girl next to me closes her eyes.

It looks like for the first time today, she's been rendered speechless.

*

I don't know who the red heels belong to.

But she's clearly very important: Harriet Manners now has cheeks so pink she looks like a little Russian doll.

"I don't know whether you're under some kind of impression that you've become invisible in the last thirteen minutes," the voice continues drily, "but you're not. I can still see you."

"Oh," Harriet says with a tiny wince, eyes closed.

"Yes, *oh. So* you may as well come out now."

There's a beat, then Harriet opens her eyes and looks directly at me so I clamp my eyes shut once more for a moment. "Thanks for sharing the table," she whispers.

Then she clambers awkwardly back out, leaving my stale chewing gum offering lying on the floor.

Probably for the best.

I suspect it would have been totally inedible.

"What are you *doing,* Harriet?"

Instinctively, I shuffle to the right and lean towards them so I can hear better. The girl's voice is a bit deeper and huskier than Harriet's, but it's strong, warm and direct.

"I... It's not what it—"

"I can't believe this. I *know* you don't like shopping, Harriet, and I *know* you didn't want to come today, but hiding under *this* table... I mean of all the tables..."

There's a silence while I lean a little further, trying to figure out what's happening.

I'm clearly not the only one.

"Well?" the voice says with a small wobble. "What's going on, Harriet?"

A throat clears. "I was... looking for unusual... table joints. For woodwork... homework."

"Huh?"

"Woodwork homework. They said... local craft can be very interesting... and we had to look in other parts of the country. Like... Birmingham."

"What?"

"So I thought... from a distance that this particular table looked very solid. In terms of construction. And I thought I'd have a closer look. You know. From... underneath."

"And?"

"A-and?" Harriet stammers. "And what?"

"What were they? What kind of table joints? I mean, you were under there quite a long time. You must have been able to tell."

There's another long silence.

I've genuinely never heard anyone lie so badly. It's like watching someone clutching at apples as they fall out of a tree: they're just basically smacking Harriet on the head one by one.

A sudden wave of protectiveness rushes through me.

I have to do *something*.

"I think that..." Harriet mumbles as she grabs for another imaginary apple. "They're..."

"They're dovetail," I say, abruptly clambering out.

"Nick!" Wilbur declares. "*There* you are! How many more of you are there under there?"

Weirdly enough, the girl who isn't Harriet is also wearing a football kit.

She's about an inch taller than Harriet and dark-skinned, with dark, long hair, a strong nose and long-lashed, narrow brown eyes. There's no doubt about it: she's good-looking. I just don't think it would translate well on camera, and – judging by the way he's gazing at a sparkly balloon on the neighbouring stall – Wilbur obviously doesn't either.

And as I glance at Harriet's horrified face I realise that's exactly the problem.

I finally understand what's happening here.

"Dovetail?" her pretty friend says, frowning and glancing at me, then at Wilbur, then at Harriet again.

"Yep," I say as firmly as possible, trying to subtly block the table and flashing her a bright smile in an attempt to distract her from the half-filled-out modelling forms, lying all over it. "Dovetail."

"Mmm." Harriet flicks me a grateful glance. "That's what I thought too."

Then I glance in horror at Wilbur's hand.

There are three Polaroid photos of Harriet clutched in it, just developing: one eye shut in two of them.

I pointedly clear my throat but it's too late: the brunette has spotted them. She makes a sudden, heartbreaking sob and Harriet's face crumples.

"Oh *no*, Nat," she says desperately, taking a step forward and reaching for her. "I didn't…"

"*No*," the pretty friend says, sharply blocking Harriet with a hand.

Her eyes fill with tears.

And, with a smooth, swift spin, she twists and jumps off the stage into the crowd of girls.

Leaving Harriet standing behind her.

*

We each have our own language.

Our own way of thinking, of talking to ourselves, of making sense of the world and putting it in order. A narration style that is ours and ours alone.

That's why some of us connect and some of us don't.

Because even though we can only live in our own heads, sometimes – every now and then – we meet a person we can talk to without speaking at all: whose story we can read, without even trying.

And as I watch this girl's face, quivering in front of me – as I feel her myriad of emotions, starting to tug through me – I realise that Harriet speaks a secret language I think I understand.

"Harriet…" I say slowly.

"I didn't mean to," she blurts distractedly, still staring into the crowd. "This wasn't supposed to happen."

Guilt spins through me.

I did this. This tidal wave came from me, and it's already pulling her away from – judging by their bizarre matching outfits – her best friend.

"Darling-pudding," Wilbur says, still totally oblivious. He's started grabbing the pink paper forms from the table. "We are going to launch you like a fashion rocket, honey. Whoosh! Into outer model space! You won't know what's hit you, baby-baby-mongoose! Fame and stardom, here you come!"

I scowl at him: *read the room, Wilbur.*

Harriet's eyes are getting larger. "No," she whispers, taking a step towards the edge of the stage. "You've made a mistake." She's beginning to sound almost angry. "You should have picked Nat."

"Nope, no mistake," Wilbur chirps happily, pinning the photos together. "To paraphrase *Grease*, you're the one that we want, sugarmuffin. So if you just drop your deets here, and here, and *here*..."

He thrusts the paper under her nose.

For just a fraction of a second, I see her waver: hope and need, coursing through her face. *She actually wants this*, I realise with surprise. She just didn't know she did, and she doesn't know where that desire has come from.

Something buried deep inside her wants to step out of the shadows, away from her pretty, fierce best friend and to take this kind of spotlight.

To change her life.

Then it's gone and something else comes slicing through.

Something steely, tough and inflexible.

"No," she says firmly, suddenly lifting her chin and looking us both straight in the eyes. "Thank you very much, but this isn't my dream and I don't want it. Please give it to somebody who does."

She picks the pile of coats back up.

Then she sits down on the stage and swings her legs on to the floor.

She takes a deep breath.

And before I can stop her, or even say goodbye, the girl with the green eyes takes one small glance backwards.

Then disappears.

*

There's a surfing term for what's just happened.

When you're caught inside a wave – when it's barrelling over your head and you're about to wipeout – you make a quick, evasive movement that takes you away from it and saves you just in time.

It's called a *bail*.

That's what Harriet's just done: the huge wave came and she bailed with a strength and grace I didn't have when it came for me.

I am beyond impressed right now.

"Chickpea, we're going to lose her!" Wilbur says urgently as my T-shirt gets tugged on for the second time today. "Nicholas, do something!"

I watch Harriet, trying to wade through the middle of a gang of girls who have no intention of stepping out of the way, with her mass of puffy coats and flailing red curls caught on somebody's handbag.

"Just let her go," I say quietly.

I'd rather she was happy even if it means I don't see her again.

"But," Wilbur stutters. "But… I don't understand what just happened. Nicholas, she's my *winner.*"

"She certainly is," a somewhat nasal voice that sounds like the owner has a persistent cold says from behind us. "Of many things, actually. The biology award last year. Maths club in Year 9 and a debate competition just last month. Then there was that yellow teddy at the fair when she was eleven although *strictly* speaking I'm pretty sure she knocked the coconut off its post with a foul throw, although the evidence is circumstantial."

Wilbur and I turn round.

There's a boy standing behind us: only a little shorter than me, with fluffy blonde hair tufting out in every direction and a red T-shirt that reads **THERE'S NO PLACE LIKE 127.0.0.1**.

I frown. "And you are...?"

"You'll find out in due course," he says in a knowingly mysterious voice. "Let's just say I am epic and usually three steps behind Harriet Manners."

"That doesn't sound healthy," I joke.

"Actually you'd be surprised at how much exercise is involved," he disagrees chirpily. "I have a *very* low resting heart rate."

Then he reaches into his rucksack and pulls out a notepad and pen. "Here." He starts scribbling on it. "This is Harriet Manners' home phone number, as well as her fax and email. Her stepmother is called Annabel and her father is Richard. She also has a dog called Hugo, but you're not going to be able to speak to him if you call. He's *rubbish* on the phone."

I can feel my mouth start to twitch again.

Even her *friends* are funny.

Then he hands over a couple of numbers with:

THE MANNERS FAMILY

written neatly on top.

Wilbur grabs it victoriously and kisses it. "Yessssss," he says, punching the air. "In your *face*, Stephanie."

"You're going to want to call," the boy says decidedly. "She's going to change her mind and your life will never be the same again."

Then – with what appears to be an awkwardly executed wink over his shoulder – the boy drops to the floor and rolls behind the stand.

Wilbur and I stare at each other.

Then at the piece of paper.

Then at the redhead, finally emerging from the crowd: unruly curls bobbing into the distance.

A surge of happiness rushes through me.

You know what?

This isn't my choice: it's hers. This is her fork in the

road, and whether she takes it or not is up to her. It's not for me to try and control. Something tells me that whatever happens next, she'll be able to handle it.

Although that doesn't mean I can't be there beside her.

Or try to be, anyway.

"You know what?" Wilbur says happily, kissing the paper again, before folding it up and carefully slipping it into his shirt pocket. "Nikolai, I think that's her. I think we've just found our girl."

I watch as the last strand of her bright hair disappears round the corner. Something's starting to tell me I probably won't quit modelling just yet. I might give it a little while longer, after all.

A grin starts to stretch across my face.

"Yup," I say as the wave begins to crest and I start speeding through the air. "I think we just did."

Acknowledgements

A book takes an army, and I'm incredibly lucky to have the most amazing one behind me. Thank you, as always, to everyone at HarperCollins. Particularly to Kate, Lizzie, Ruth and Rachel: for having faith in me, and for encouraging me to have faith in myself. Thanks to Paul, Simon, Nicola, Sam and Hannah, for continuing to bring Harriet to readers in the UK, and to Carla and her team for spreading the word internationally. Thanks to Kate and Elisabetta and everyone on Team Geek who quietly slaves away behind the scenes: Brigid, JP, Victoria, Caroline and Amy, marshmallows with my face on them will never be enough.

And thanks to my family. You love me and you've never let me forget it.

Thank you. X

See how it all began...

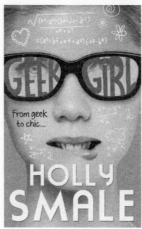

Harriet Manners knows a lot of things.

* Cats have 32 muscles in each ear
* Bluebirds can't see the colour blue
* The average person laughs 15 times per day
* Peanuts are an ingredient in dynamite

But she doesn't know why nobody at school seems to like her. So when she's offered the chance to reinvent herself, Harriet grabs it. Can she transform from geek to chic?

The geek is back!

Harriet Manners also knows:

* Humans have 70,000 thoughts per day
* Caterpillars have four thousand muscles
* The average person eats a ton of food a year
* Being a Geek + Model = a whole new set of graffiti on your belongings

But clearly she knows nothing about boys. And on a whirlwind modelling trip to Tokyo, Harriet would trade in everything she's ever learnt for just the faintest idea of what she's supposed to do next...

Geek girl goes Stateside...

Harriet Manners knows a lot of facts:

* New York is the most populous city
  in the United States
* its official motto is 'Ever Upward'
* 27% of Americans believe we never
  landed on the moon

But she has no idea about modelling Stateside. Or,
even more importantly, what to do when the big
romantic gestures aren't coming from her boyfriend...

The original geek returns...

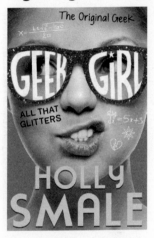

Harriet Manners has high hopes for the new school year: she's a Sixth Former now, and things are going to be different. But with Nat busy falling in love at college and Toby preoccupied with a Top Secret project, Harriet soon discovers that's not necessarily a good thing. . .

No. 1. Geek!

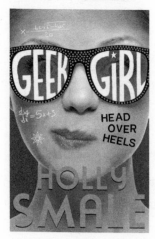

Harriet Manners knows almost every fact there is.

* Fourteen squirrels were once
detained as spies
* Snakes and Ladders and Chess were
both invented in the same country
* Astronauts' hearts become rounder in space

And for once, Harriet knows exactly how her life should go. She's got it ALL planned out. So when love is in the air, Harriet is determined to Make Things Happen! If only everyone else would stick to the script...

Has GEEK GIRL overstepped the mark, and is following the rules going to break hearts all over again?

DO NOT MISS...

The FINAL book in the bestselling, award-winning GEEK GIRL series is COMING SOON!

My name is Harriet Manners and I'll be a geek forever...

Harriet Manners knows almost every fact there is...

* Modelling isn't a sure-fire route to popularity.
* Neither is making endless lists.
* The people you love don't expect you to transform into someone else.
* Statistically you are more likely to not meet your Australian ex-boyfriend in Australia than bump into him there.

So on the trip of a lifetime Down Under Harriet's to-do lists are gone and it's Nat's time to shine! Yet with nearly-not-quite-boyfriend Jasper back home Harriet is completely unprepared to see supermodel ex Nick. Is the fashion world about to turn ugly for GEEK GIRL?

It's time for Harriet to face the future. Time to work out where her heart lies. To learn how to let go...

GEEK ★ GiRL

HEAD TO OUR FACEBOOK PAGE
f /GeekGirlSeries

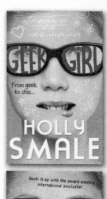

coming soon

 @HolSmale